*To Virginia*

# The HOBBIT SKETCHBOOK

## Alan Lee

HarperCollins*Publishers*

Also illustrated by Alan Lee:

CASTLES
FAERIES
THE MABINOGION
THE MOON'S REVENGE
BLACK SHIPS BEFORE TROY
THE WANDERINGS OF ODYSSEUS
THE LORD OF THE RINGS
THE HOBBIT
THE ART OF THE LORD OF THE RINGS
THE CHILDREN OF HÚRIN
TALES FROM THE PERILOUS REALM
SHAPESHIFTERS: TALES FROM OVID'S METAMORPHOSES
BEREN AND LÚTHIEN
THE WANDERER & OTHER OLD-ENGLISH POEMS
THE FALL OF GONDOLIN
THE FALL OF NÚMENOR

HarperCollins*Publishers* Ltd
1 London Bridge Street,
London SE1 9GF
www.harpercollins.co.uk

HarperCollins*Publishers*
Macken House, 39/40 Mayor Street Upper
Dublin 1, D01 C9W8, Ireland

First published by HarperCollins*Publishers* 2019

5

Copyright © Alan Lee 2019

Quotation from *The Hobbit* by J.R.R. Tolkien © The Tolkien Estate Limited 1937, 1965

Alan Lee asserts the moral right to be identified as the author of this work

☒® and 'Tolkien'® are registered trade marks
of The Tolkien Estate Limited

All sketches produced specifically during the development of *The Hobbit* film trilogy
are reproduced courtesy of New Line Productions Inc. and Warner Bros. Entertainment Inc.

A catalogue record for this book is available from the British Library

Editor: Chris Smith

ISBN: 978 0 00 822674 9

Set in Bembo and Trajan

Printed and bound in Italy by Rotolito S.p.A.

All rights reserved. No part of this publication may be reproduced, stored in a retrieval system,
or transmitted, in any form or by any means, electronic, mechanical, photocopying,
recording or otherwise, without the prior permission of the publishers.

# Contents

| | |
|---|---|
| INTRODUCTION | 8 |
| BAG END | 12 |
|    Timing | 22 |
|    Watercolour | 28 |
| THE LONE-LANDS | 30 |
|    Rivendell | 36 |
| THE MISTY MOUNTAINS | 56 |
|    Goblins | 60 |
|    Gollum | 67 |
|    Frying-Pan | 70 |
| WILDERLAND | 74 |
| MIRKWOOD | 84 |
|    Radagast | 94 |
|    Rhosgobel | 96 |
|    Dol Guldur | 102 |
|    Enchanted Stream | 112 |
|    The Caves of the Elvenking | 122 |
|    Wine Cellar | 130 |
| LAKE-TOWN | 134 |
| DALE & EREBOR | 144 |
|    Bard & Smaug | 162 |
|    The Battle of Five Armies | 176 |
|    Going Home | 188 |
| ACKNOWLEDGEMENTS | 190 |

# INTRODUCTION

I read *The Hobbit* after finishing the three volumes of *The Lord of the Rings* when I was seventeen, and on a hiatus from art school. I also illustrated the books and worked on the films in that same order. In some ways it might have been even more pleasurable to have come across *The Hobbit* first, and then experienced that deeper immersion into Middle-earth as a further exploration. It's odd to think that, fresh from the slopes of Mount Doom, you may know more about the implications of some of the events in *The Hobbit* than the author did when he wrote it. Of course, Tolkien did go back to *The Hobbit* to make some revisions for later editions after *The Lord of the Rings* was published, so the transition either way is seamless.

That prior knowledge didn't make the book any less exciting or beautiful; the unfolding of events doesn't become less magical if we already have some inkling of what may happen, because the pleasure is in the brilliance of the storytelling and the world that is evoked.

For me, Middle-earth is inextricably linked to the wider world of folklore and myth that I grew up with, through discovering as a child the Oxford Books of myth and legend and retellings of the Arthurian, Celtic and Norse myths in libraries and, as I read the books, to the landscape around me. That is the magic of stories – as we listen or read we are constructing the imagery from our own raw materials.

Illustrating Tolkien's works wasn't part of a long-term plan, or even an ambition – I think it seemed out of range as I was starting work as an illustrator in 1970 – but I did want to involve myself in myths and legends in some way and found my way there through meeting a remarkable series of people. David Larkin, art director at Pan, had given me my first commissions, and through him I met the wonderful Ian and Betty Ballantine (they had produced the first authorized paperback edition of *The Lord of the Rings* in the US) and they published *Faeries* and *Castles* – the UK edition of which was published by Unwin Hyman. Since I had included a few Middle-earth edifices in the book, Jane Johnson, editor at that company, put those into their Tolkien calendar. And followed that by suggesting I illustrate *The Lord of the Rings*. This was fairly well received and I went on to illustrate *The Hobbit* and, with the support of Christopher Tolkien and the Tolkien Estate, the three 'Great Tales' of the First Age of Middle-earth. All of the books published in the last twenty years have been proposed by the very patient and insightful Chris Smith and David Brawn at Harper Collins.

All of this led on to work with the brilliant New Zealand film-makers, Peter Jackson and Fran Walsh, and a friendly collaboration with a kindred spirit, John Howe. None of these were chance meetings, of course, but staying awake to the possibility of adventure and being easygoing, even if you are not easily found, played a part.

My thanks to all of them, and to you!

*Alan Lee*

# Bag End

Every good fairy story involves a Call to Adventure: a choice made between a safe and predictable existence and the lure of the unknown. I wanted to make Bilbo's home, and its surrounding gardens and landscapes, as beautiful and comfortable as possible – a place that anyone would find it hard to wrench themselves away from. Some of the domestic details in this picture are taken from my own home, and the view is based on local vistas of woods, fields and hills, with Dartmoor's uplands in the background.

# Bag End

Every good fairy story involves a Call to Adventure: a choice made between a safe and predictable existence and the lure of the unknown. I wanted to make Bilbo's home, and its surrounding gardens and landscapes, as beautiful and comfortable as possible – a place that anyone would find it hard to wrench themselves away from. Some of the domestic details in this picture are taken from my own home, and the view is based on local vistas of woods, fields and hills, with Dartmoor's uplands in the background.

These other dwellings in Hobbiton are more humble, and nestle into the folds of the valleys rather than sitting prominently on the brow of a hill. They are inspired by vernacular architecture, constructed of cob, stone, oak timbers and brickwork. Much of the inspiration for their design comes from the low, thatched cottages of Devon and some of the other English shires.

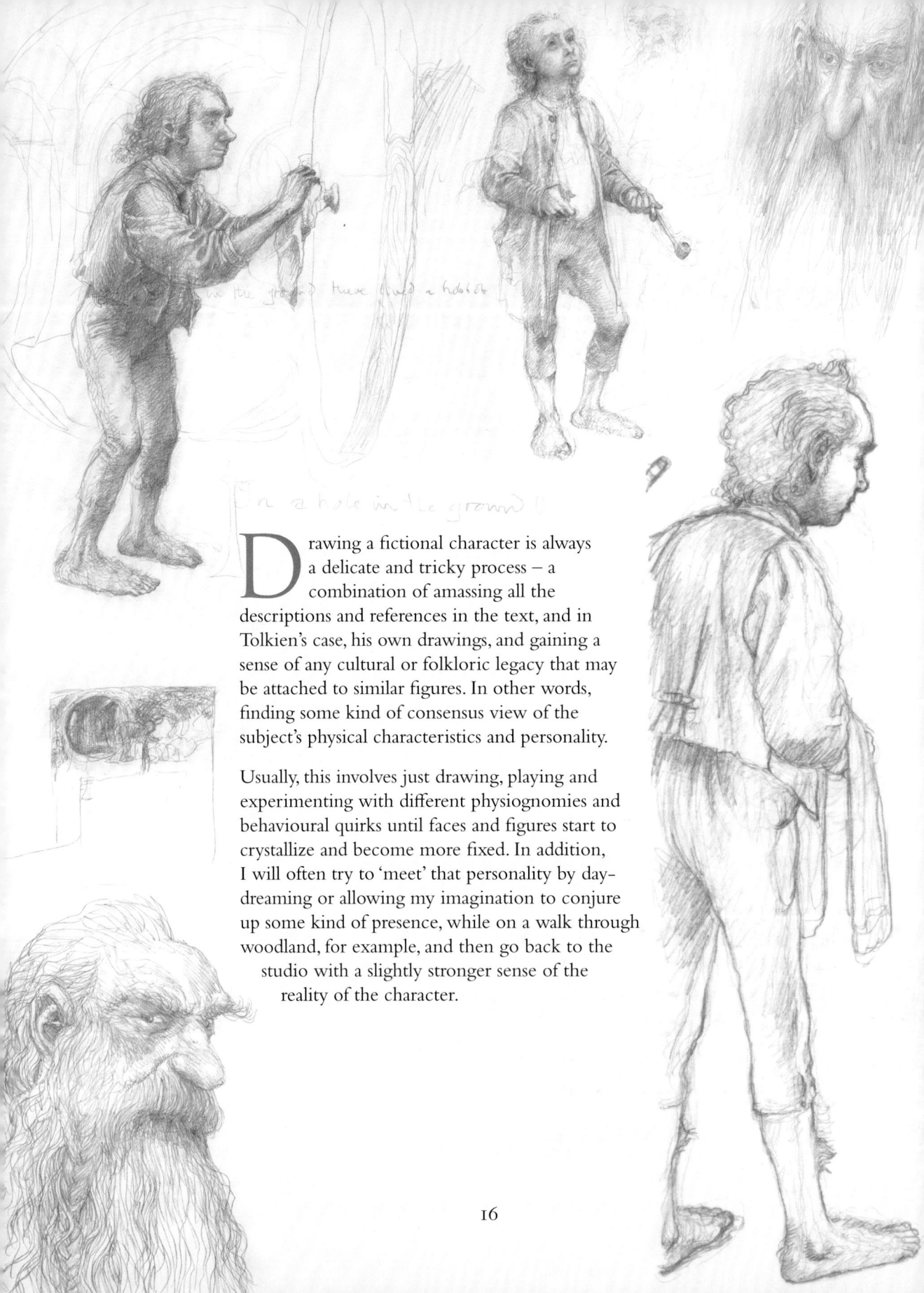

Drawing a fictional character is always a delicate and tricky process – a combination of amassing all the descriptions and references in the text, and in Tolkien's case, his own drawings, and gaining a sense of any cultural or folkloric legacy that may be attached to similar figures. In other words, finding some kind of consensus view of the subject's physical characteristics and personality.

Usually, this involves just drawing, playing and experimenting with different physiognomies and behavioural quirks until faces and figures start to crystallize and become more fixed. In addition, I will often try to 'meet' that personality by day-dreaming or allowing my imagination to conjure up some kind of presence, while on a walk through woodland, for example, and then go back to the studio with a slightly stronger sense of the reality of the character.

Drawing fourteen characters is even trickier, but it's good to get them all into at least one picture, even if it gets a little cramped. Reading carefully and gleaning any description, no matter how insignificant, is important, but for some of the dwarves we know little more about their looks than the colour of their hoods.

The author creates a small problem for an illustrator when he describes Gandalf's eyebrows as being so long that they project beyond the brim of his shady hat. Having to choose between keeping his eyebrows and his iconic wizard's hat, I chose the latter.

As Bilbo goes to sleep, having spontaneously agreed to become the burglar, therefore in the most dangerous role, on the expedition to the Lonely Mountain, he can still hear Thorin singing about his ancient home, of the mountains, caverns and a gleaming hoard. This for me is one of the most beautiful passages in the book. The description of the shadow of Gandalf's beard on the wall, the room darkening as the deep voices sing of jewels like stars and enchanted gold, evokes that essential longing that lies at the heart of Norse and Old English poetry.

*Far over the Misty Mountains cold*
*To dungeons deep and caverns old*
*We must away ere break of day*
*To seek the pale enchanted gold*

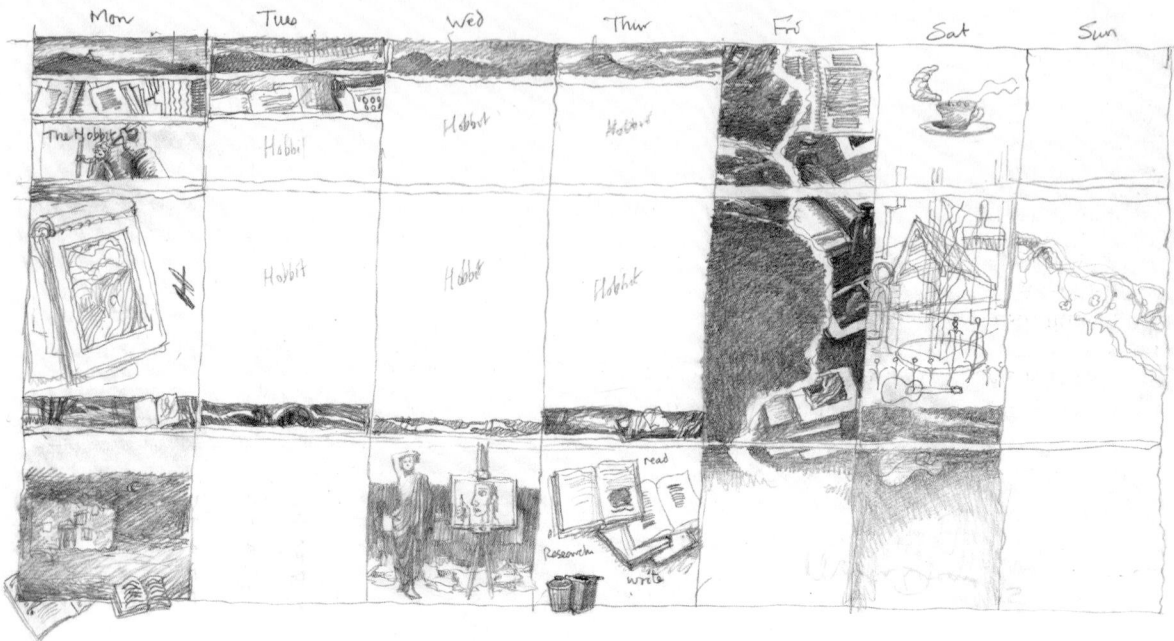

# Timing

I'm not the most well-organized person, and find that work usually expands to overflow the time I have allotted to it, to the point where it subsumes every other aspect of daily life. With each new project I make some vain attempt to set time aside for other activities and retain some balance. When starting work on my illustrated edition of *The Hobbit*, I made this weekly timetable with periods set aside for other pleasures and responsibilities. I was keen to keep working on other projects, so reserved Friday for landscape drawing or printmaking, and promised myself a walk first thing in the morning and every evening. Wednesday evening was devoted to a regular life-drawing group that I hosted in my studio. Like a New Year's resolution, this regime lasted just a few weeks before the illustrations themselves rebelled against this attempt to contain them and, demanding my full-time attention, we fell back into the familiar pattern of working late into the night in order to meet the dates set out in the contract.

I am usually over-optimistic about the time any project will take to complete, but I also want every picture to take a natural course and as much time as is needed to finish it without hurrying. Shortcuts taken to speed up the process often lead to having to restart the painting.

The first stages are usually small thumbnail studies or larger, very loose charcoal sketches. Sometimes there will be pages of random doodles before something relating to the subject will appear. This is to allow the less conscious part of my mind to play with ideas before a more rational refining process sets in. These initial sketches often have a quality that is hard to retain in the working drawings that follow, as they become more defined and heavily worked.

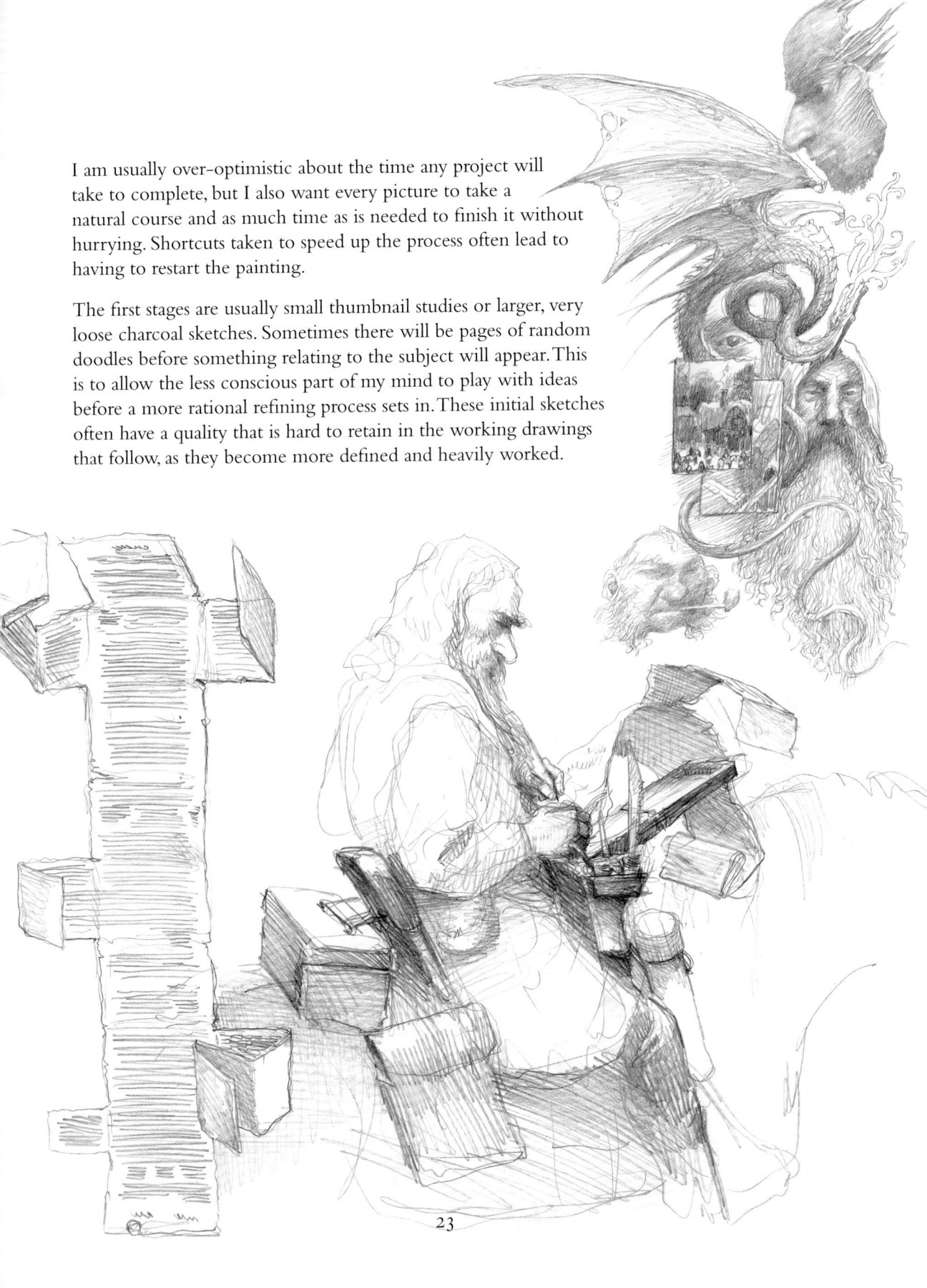

There will be separate pencil studies of different parts of the picture, and anything that I will need to bear in mind while completing it. If I am searching the internet or reference books for costumes or architecture, I will sketch quick copies of the most useful examples so that it is all available at a glance. Having photographic reference is useful, but we see an object in a different way after having looked at it closely enough to draw it, and it becomes more firmly fixed in the imagination.

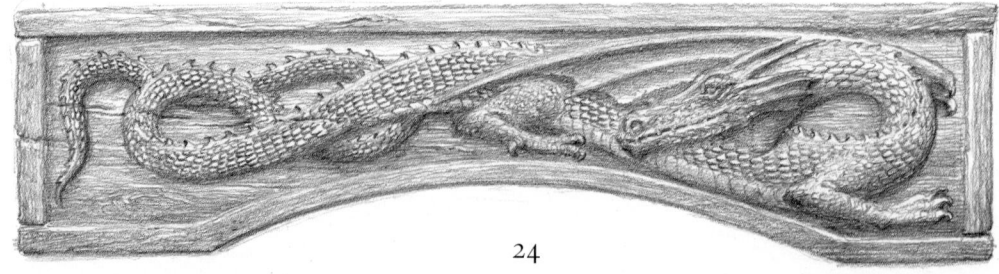

I am usually over-optimistic about the time any project will take to complete, but I also want every picture to take a natural course and as much time as is needed to finish it without hurrying. Shortcuts taken to speed up the process often lead to having to restart the painting.

The first stages are usually small thumbnail studies or larger, very loose charcoal sketches. Sometimes there will be pages of random doodles before something relating to the subject will appear. This is to allow the less conscious part of my mind to play with ideas before a more rational refining process sets in. These initial sketches often have a quality that is hard to retain in the working drawings that follow, as they become more defined and heavily worked.

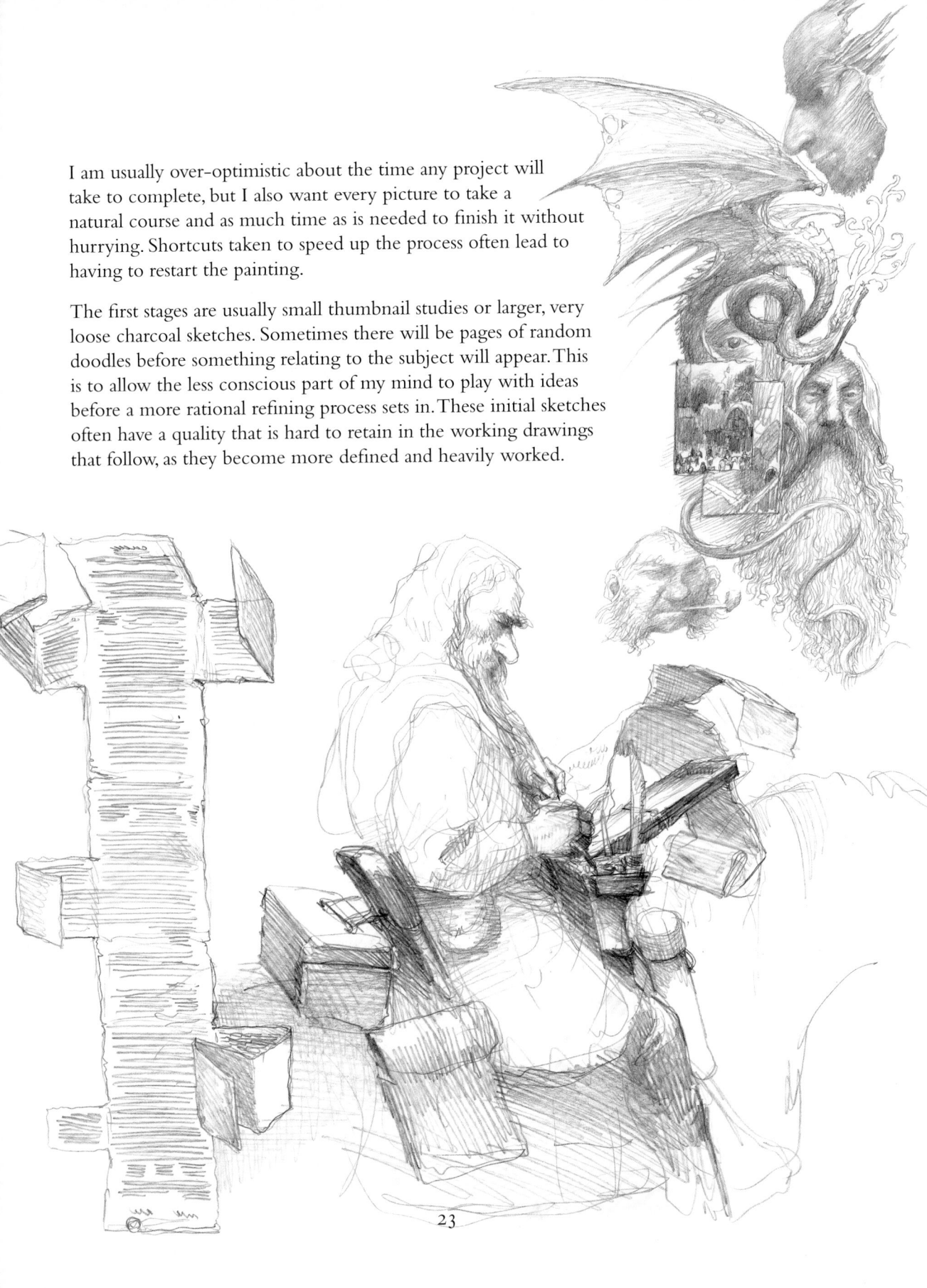

There will be separate pencil studies of different parts of the picture, and anything that I will need to bear in mind while completing it. If I am searching the internet or reference books for costumes or architecture, I will sketch quick copies of the most useful examples so that it is all available at a glance. Having photographic reference is useful, but we see an object in a different way after having looked at it closely enough to draw it, and it becomes more firmly fixed in the imagination.

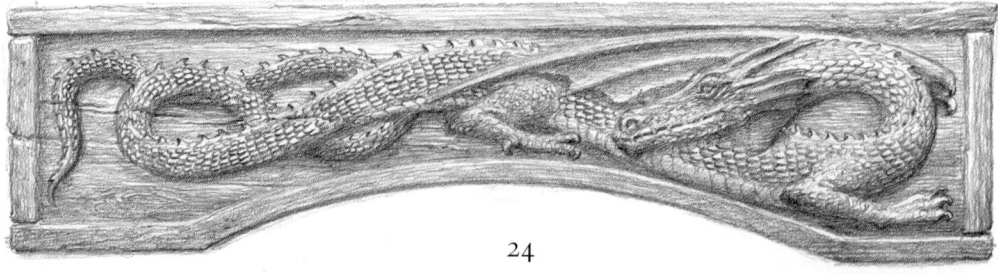

I may go for a walk and make studies of landscapes so that a drawing made later from the imagination will be more believable. It isn't that the earlier sketches are copied into the image, but that something of their solidity and texture persists. It is good to have the drawings to refer to but the experience of looking very intently at something over a period of time is more valuable.

I will also draw from life as much as possible, asking friends and family to get into character so that I can make some quick sketches. I'll take photos as well, especially for the more dramatic moments.

If there are to be several drawings of the same character or creature, I may make a small Plasticine model and draw from that. This gives me an opportunity to see the same forms from many angles, and to vary the lighting.

Most of the time, however, I find myself drawing and composing pictures entirely from the imagination, and trying to get as close as I can to the images and characters conjured by the text, rather than bothering my friends by spending too much time examining their features for traces of elven lineage.

A colour illustration will be preceded by a dozen or so pencil drawings working through different possibilities before the essential elements of a final drawing on a sheet of layout paper are transferred onto the stretched watercolour paper. One way of doing this is to place a sheet of graphite-covered tissue paper between them and draw over the composition with a very hard and sharp pencil to transfer the outlines.

# Watercolour

I think of watercolour as a means of developing a drawing, rather than as a way of rendering an idea as a fixed and permanent statement. Even though it may be very detailed, there is something in the mutable nature of the medium that makes it a further stage in a shifting interpretation of the story. Drawings suggest possibilities rather than exact definitions, and allowing the random and semi-accidental nature of watercolour has a similar effect, in the hope that it will be a gentle encouragement to the viewer's own imagination.

I try to keep the under-drawing to a minimum and allow washes of colour to merge and find their own edges, especially when tackling the more organic areas of the picture. Clouds, rocky hillsides, trees and the misty atmosphere that binds them together are expressed through working wet into wet – adding colour or water, then pulling the colour out with a dry brush, before leaving that part of the picture to settle and dry. The results may differ a little from what I originally had in mind, and will influence subsequent washes, so the whole process is a dialogue with the materials. When it goes well it is as though the subject is being revealed through dispersing layers of mist; the whole thing starts as an atmospheric effect which gradually clarifies, often leaving pockets of mist or shreds of cloud clinging to the more heavily worked and textured rocks and other landscape elements.

The colours I use most frequently are French Ultramarine, Cobalt Blue, Light Red, Indian Yellow and Neutral Tint. The greyish tones that

predominate are usually optical greys, created by mixing or overlaying complementary colours, which leaves a livelier surface. The physical qualities of the paint are important: a mixture of French Ultramarine and Burnt Sienna will leave a granulated wash, the heavier pigments settling into the texture of the paper.

I use very little white; the strongest highlights have to be planned for in the initial washes as they will be left as untouched paper. One of the techniques I use to create texture in those first washes is to sprinkle salt into the wet paint. As the wash dries, those individual grains will absorb some of the liquid, leaving textures that resemble lichen, flowers, or the roughness of rock. I will often explore these techniques in little experimental doodles around the border of the stretched paper, as each type, weight and surface of the watercolour paper will have its own qualities which will affect whatever I have planned for it.

There are some good, reliable papers still being made, but I get more pleasure from using older handmade papers. I have a few remaining sheets of paper that were made in the 1950s that are delightful to work on but I use those very sparingly now. The choice of paper is a big consideration when starting a new piece: a rough-textured surface will be great for producing big, luscious washes, but can be difficult to work when some detail is needed. I often resort to smoothing out small areas of the surface by burnishing with the back of a spoon, so that I can work with a finer brush on a small figure in the landscape. A smooth Hot-pressed paper makes it possible to create very delicate, subtle effects and detail but is less suited to scenes with a lot of depth and dramatic skies, so for these I generally work on 'Not', or cold-pressed, papers.

# The Lone-lands

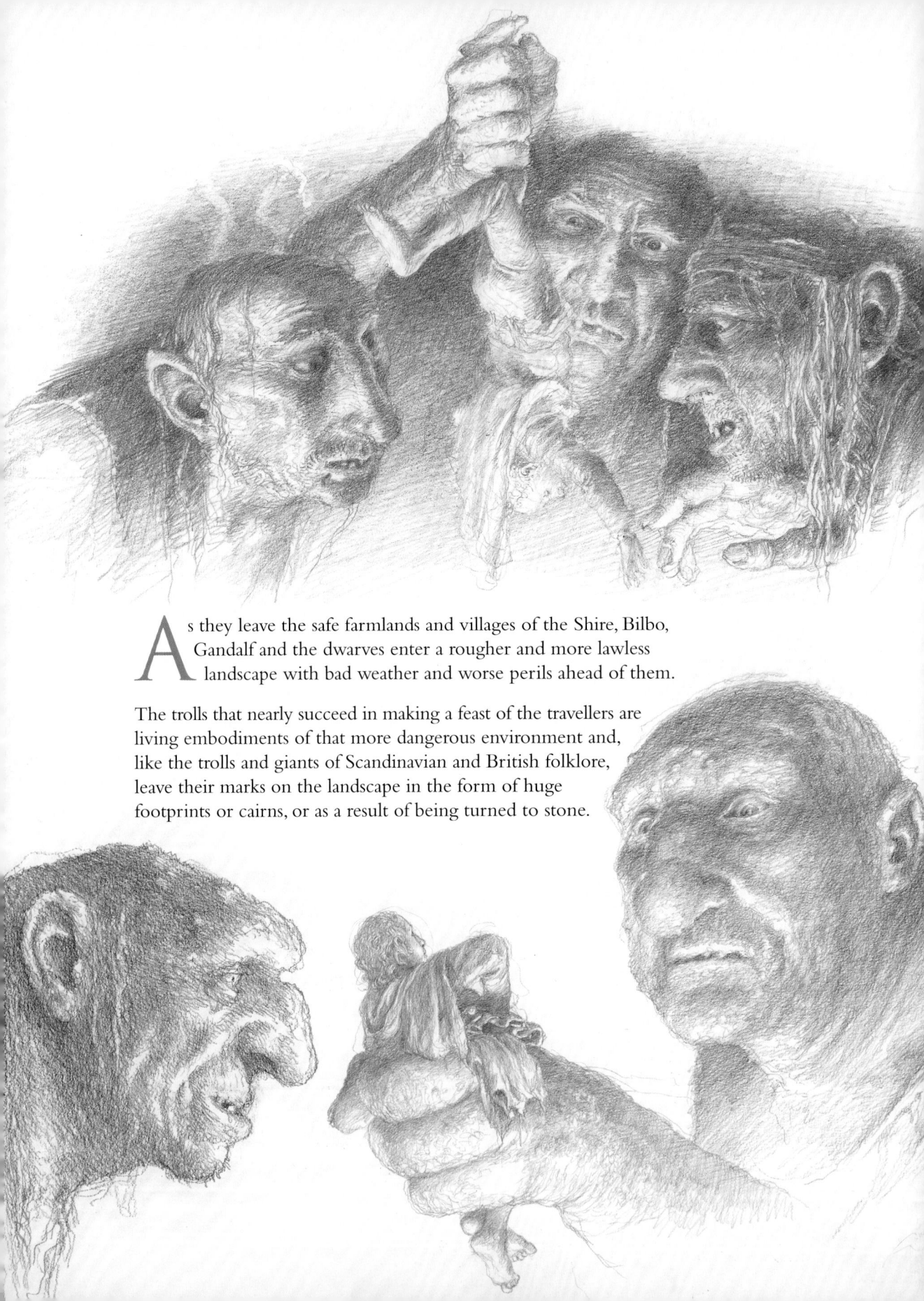

As they leave the safe farmlands and villages of the Shire, Bilbo, Gandalf and the dwarves enter a rougher and more lawless landscape with bad weather and worse perils ahead of them.

The trolls that nearly succeed in making a feast of the travellers are living embodiments of that more dangerous environment and, like the trolls and giants of Scandinavian and British folklore, leave their marks on the landscape in the form of huge footprints or cairns, or as a result of being turned to stone.

One of these, close to where I live, is Bowerman's Nose, said to be the petrified remains of a legendary hunter, while a nearby craggy outcrop, Hound Tor, is named after the devilish pack of hounds that hunted souls at night, turned to stone by the rising sun. Tolkien gives his trolls names and personalities, but Gandalf's trickery ensures that they revert to their true nature, and that their lair can be found – a cave full of stolen goods, yielding more treasure for the dwarves and weapons for Gandalf, Thorin and Bilbo.

# Rivendell

In this wild landscape Rivendell is a secret sanctuary; hidden away in a valley, Elrond's Last Homely House is a refuge and the repository of an elven culture which is slowly disappearing from Middle-earth. It is also, thanks to Tolkien's powerful imagination and evocative descriptions, for the reader or occasional illustrator an invitation to create their own version of an ideal way of life.

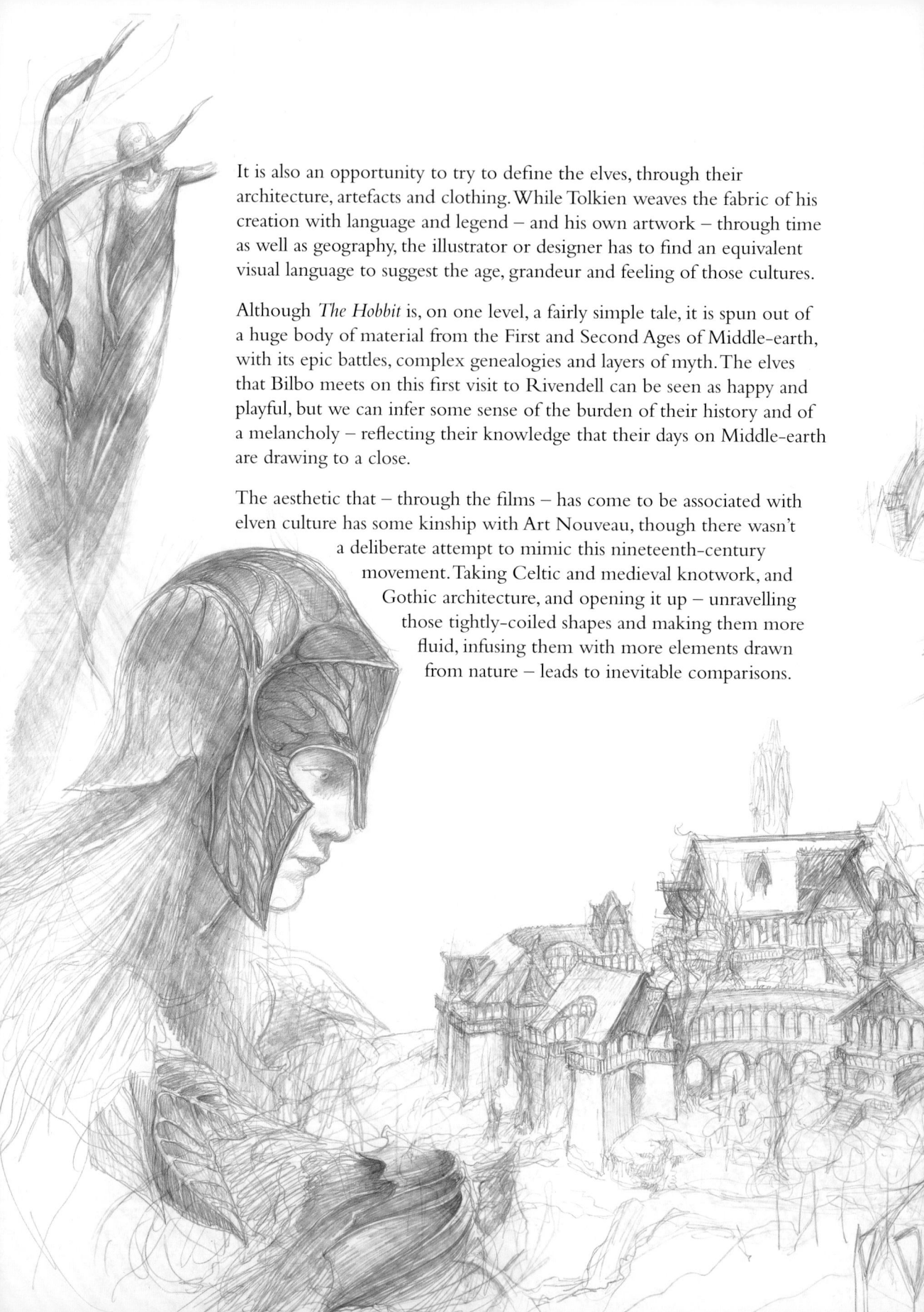

It is also an opportunity to try to define the elves, through their architecture, artefacts and clothing. While Tolkien weaves the fabric of his creation with language and legend – and his own artwork – through time as well as geography, the illustrator or designer has to find an equivalent visual language to suggest the age, grandeur and feeling of those cultures.

Although *The Hobbit* is, on one level, a fairly simple tale, it is spun out of a huge body of material from the First and Second Ages of Middle-earth, with its epic battles, complex genealogies and layers of myth. The elves that Bilbo meets on this first visit to Rivendell can be seen as happy and playful, but we can infer some sense of the burden of their history and of a melancholy – reflecting their knowledge that their days on Middle-earth are drawing to a close.

The aesthetic that – through the films – has come to be associated with elven culture has some kinship with Art Nouveau, though there wasn't a deliberate attempt to mimic this nineteenth-century movement. Taking Celtic and medieval knotwork, and Gothic architecture, and opening it up – unravelling those tightly-coiled shapes and making them more fluid, infusing them with more elements drawn from nature – leads to inevitable comparisons.

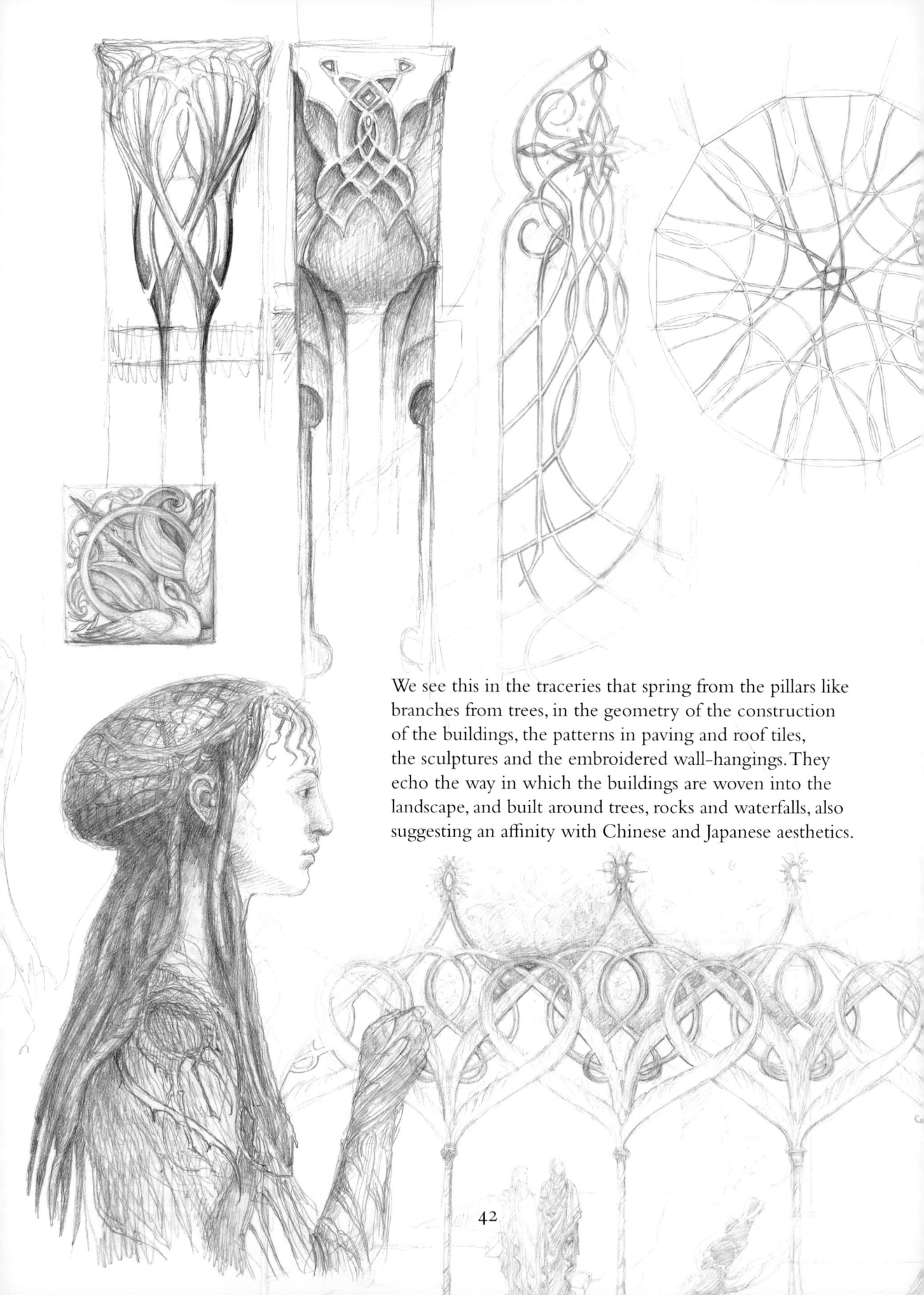

We see this in the traceries that spring from the pillars like branches from trees, in the geometry of the construction of the buildings, the patterns in paving and roof tiles, the sculptures and the embroidered wall-hangings. They echo the way in which the buildings are woven into the landscape, and built around trees, rocks and waterfalls, also suggesting an affinity with Chinese and Japanese aesthetics.

This affinity also informs the costumes of the elves, and, when we see them as warriors, their armour and weapons, banners and other martial heirlooms. Weta Workshop's design and manufacture of these artefacts, and their intense attention to detail and functionality, strengthens the links with Oriental cultures.

While working on the films of *The Hobbit* and *The Lord of the Rings*, there were many places which we explored conceptually but that didn't get further than the drawing or model-making stage. The scripts and storylines were in a continual state of flux and drawings were a good way of helping the director find a route through the story.

There was one idea that some of the conversations between Elrond and Gandalf might take place in an aviary, following the notion that one of Elrond's falcons had played a part in guiding the travellers to the sanctuary.

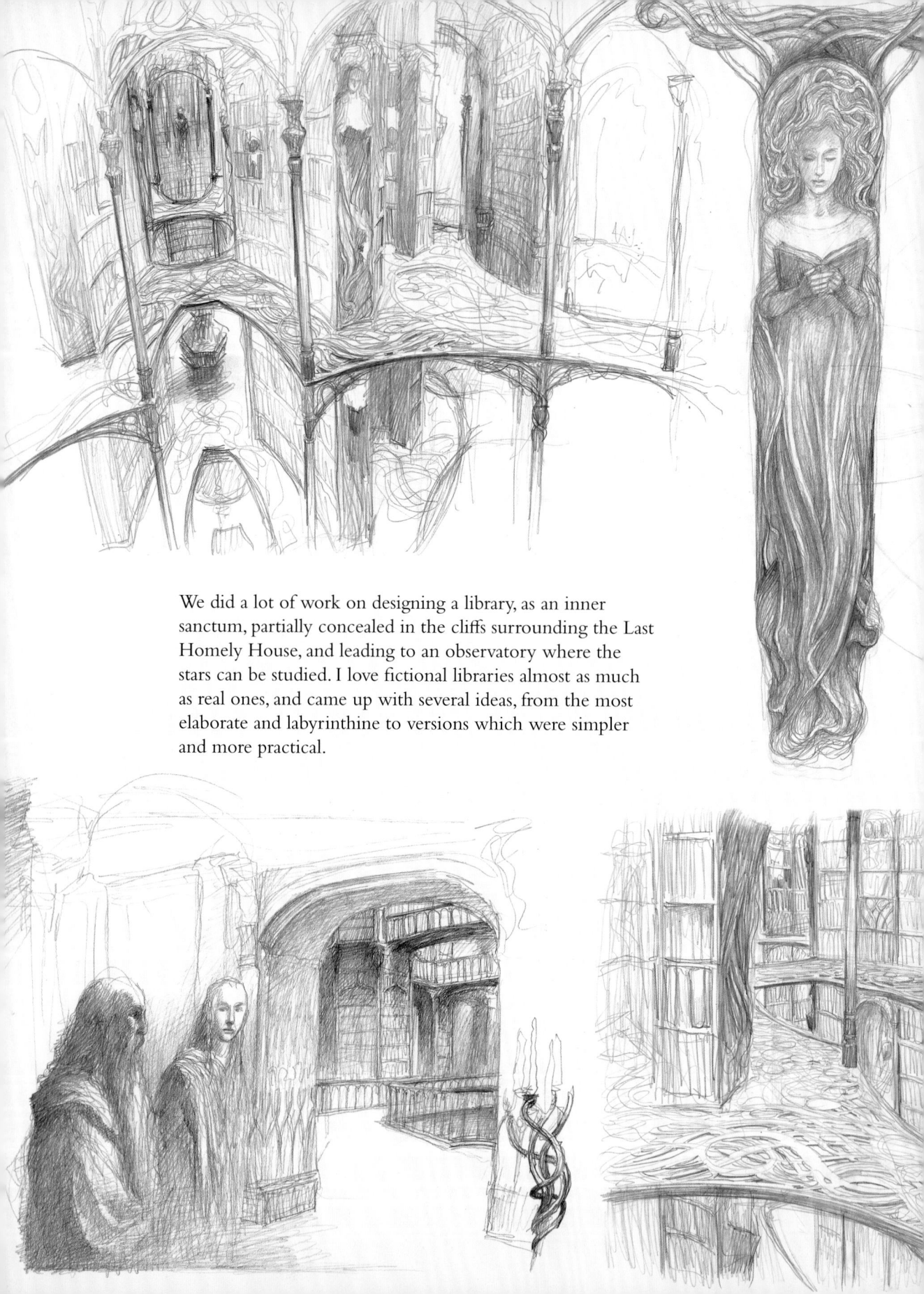

We did a lot of work on designing a library, as an inner sanctum, partially concealed in the cliffs surrounding the Last Homely House, and leading to an observatory where the stars can be studied. I love fictional libraries almost as much as real ones, and came up with several ideas, from the most elaborate and labyrinthine to versions which were simpler and more practical.

The images on these pages show how natural light could filter down through the fretwork steps and platforms of this vertical library and scriptorium, to be supplemented by some lamp-bearing carved figures.

The overall theme that sustains our image of Rivendell is that it is a place where all who find it will enjoy whatever brings them most happiness, whether it is music, books and learning, companionship or peace and the beauty of nature. As such, it comes close to representing an idea of an earthly paradise, albeit a temporary substitute for the real paradise that the elves yearn for.

In re-creating Rivendell for the *Hobbit* films, we wanted to make it recognizably the same place that we had created both as a miniature and as full-size sets for *The Lord of the Rings*, but would offer variety by adding new buildings and bringing the travellers in through a different entrance – which we could imagine to have been tucked out of sight in the views of the whole structure seen before.

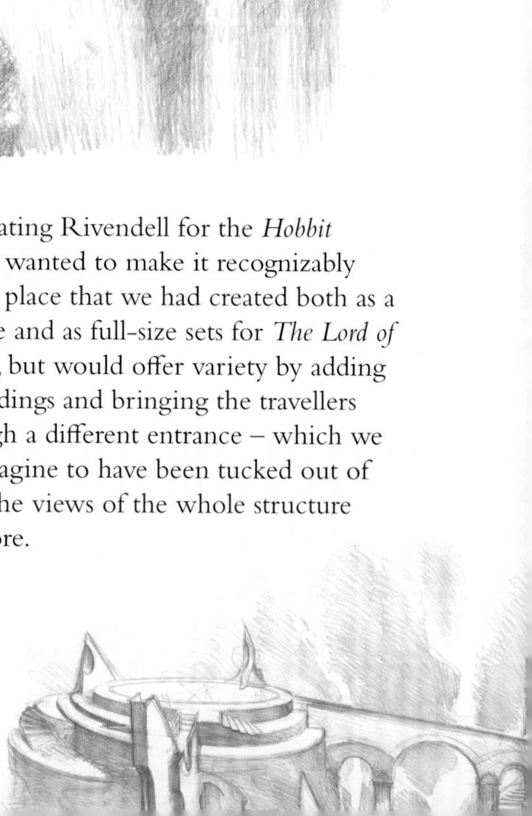

One of the new buildings was the Council Chamber, in which Galadriel and Saruman make an appearance as part of the White Council. It was placed quite prominently in the valley at the back of the Last Homely House, and was a development of a smaller, single-storey building – a rotunda – which was part of the miniature seen in *The Fellowship of the Ring*. I doubt that many viewers would have noticed it in that context, but I derive a little satisfaction from knowing that its original purpose was as a setting for the Council of Elrond, before that scene was moved to an external part of Elrond's chamber. It would now serve a similar function in *The Hobbit* – as a place where we witness being discussed some of the wider issues surrounding the Quest of Erebor before our heroes continue their journey.

# The Misty Mountains

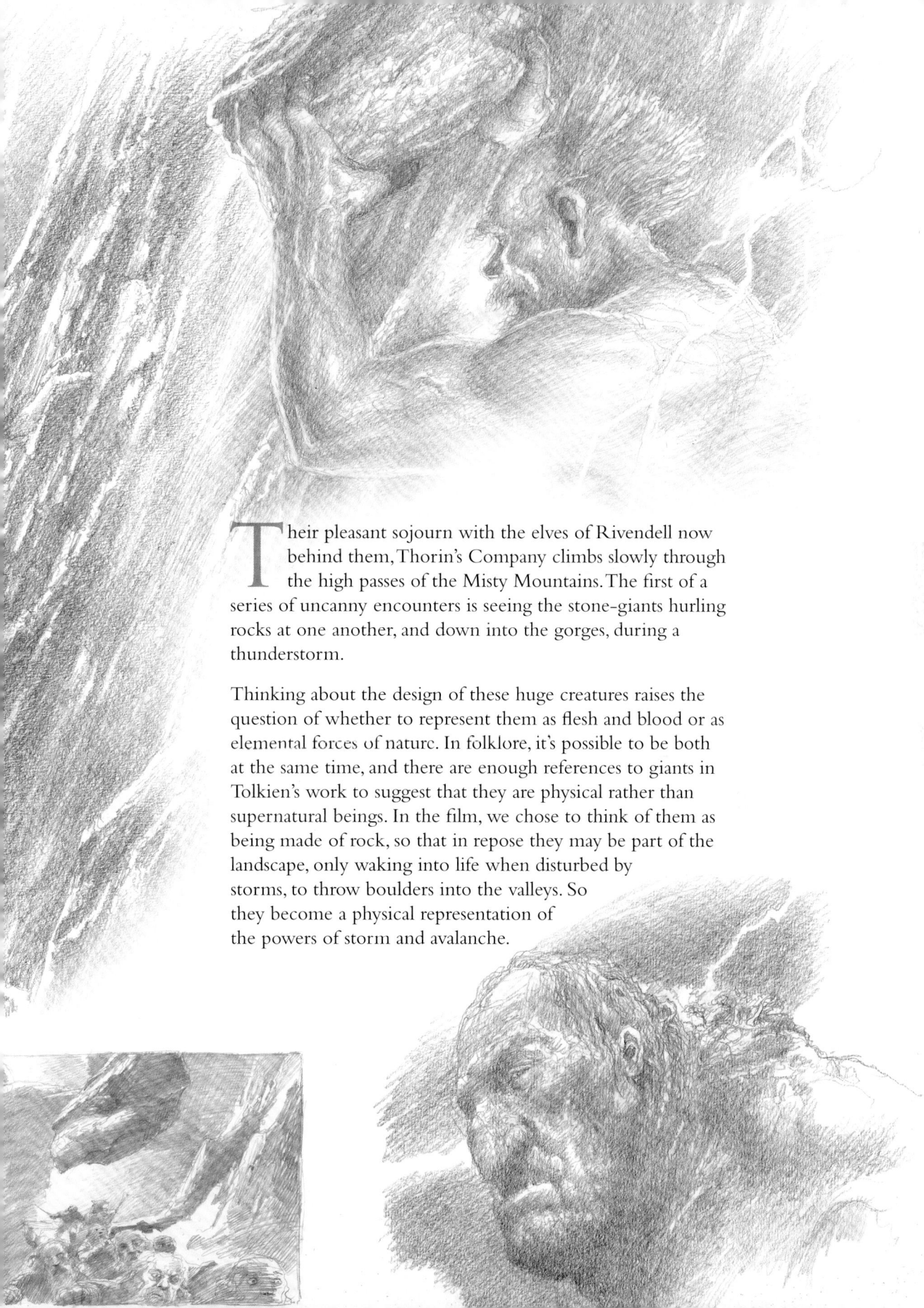

Their pleasant sojourn with the elves of Rivendell now behind them, Thorin's Company climbs slowly through the high passes of the Misty Mountains. The first of a series of uncanny encounters is seeing the stone-giants hurling rocks at one another, and down into the gorges, during a thunderstorm.

Thinking about the design of these huge creatures raises the question of whether to represent them as flesh and blood or as elemental forces of nature. In folklore, it's possible to be both at the same time, and there are enough references to giants in Tolkien's work to suggest that they are physical rather than supernatural beings. In the film, we chose to think of them as being made of rock, so that in repose they may be part of the landscape, only waking into life when disturbed by storms, to throw boulders into the valleys. So they become a physical representation of the powers of storm and avalanche.

# Goblins

Goblins, or orcs, as he referred to them later, have a more well-established place in Tolkien's legendarium as the servants of Morgoth, and Sauron. Whether created by these demonic spirits, or transformed by them through years of torment, or born from primeval heat and slime, their role is as the villainous and blindly obedient foot soldiers of evil. Here, though, as the Great Goblin's minions, they also add some dark humour.

I've been drawing goblins of one type or another for many years, though more often they are the individual characters we find in folklore inhabiting particular unnerving locations, such as pools, caves or mines. Though often malevolent, they can usually be placated with small gifts, or appropriate actions.

Creating the varieties of ferocious orcs, goblins and their allies was a major part of the work done by Weta Workshop and Weta Digital throughout the production of the films. I wasn't too involved with this aspect, concentrating instead on the places they inhabit. In the case of the Goblin King's realm we wanted to add even more danger and drama into the environment, with cave interiors of deeply striated and eroded rocky chasms, supporting flimsy structures of wood and salvaged or stolen goods that could collapse in the chaos of the captives' escape.

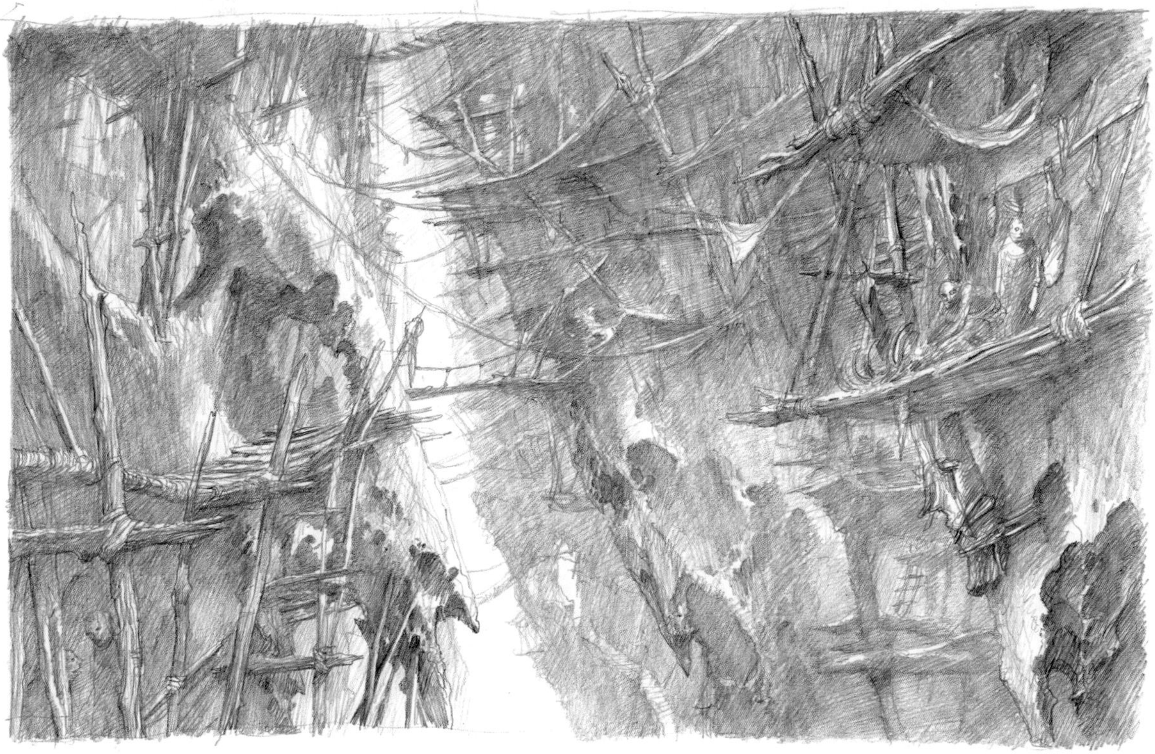

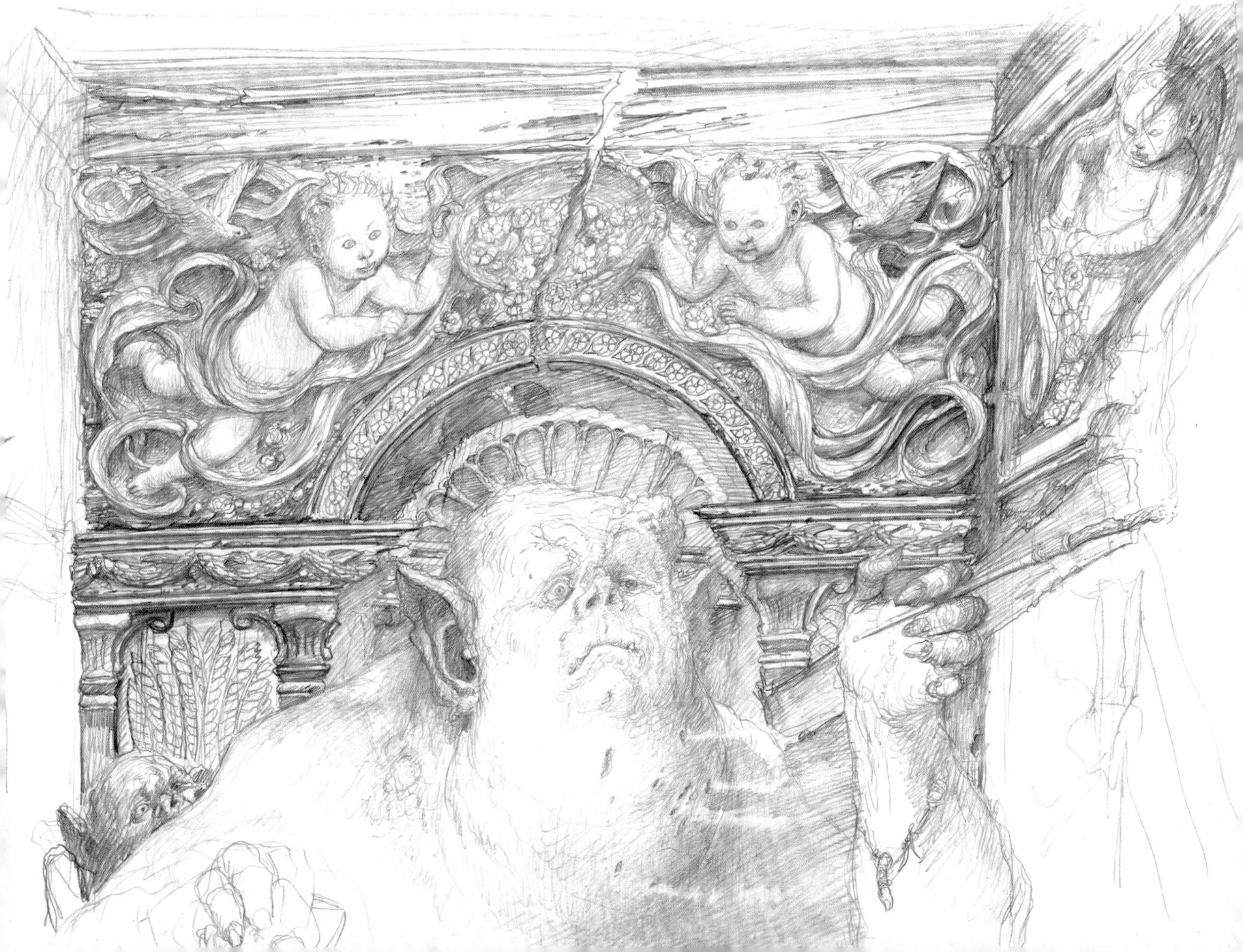

## Gollum

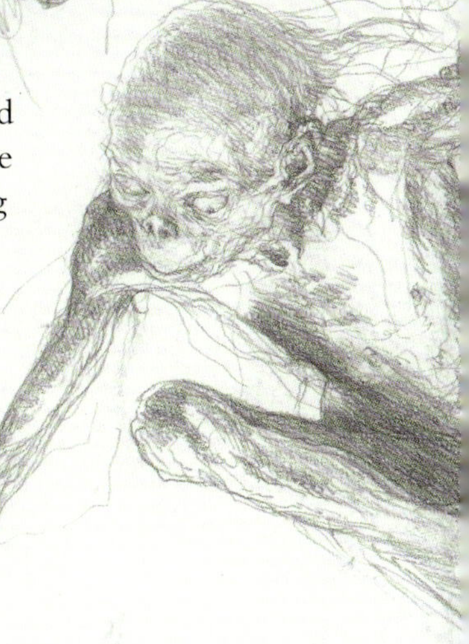

Though the finding of the Ring, the encounter with Gollum and the riddle contest would go on to become increasingly meaningful as Tolkien developed his 'new Hobbit' – *The Lord of the Rings* – into the vast epic that it became, he didn't know at the time that the Ring had any further power beyond making its wearer invisible, or any connection with the Necromancer/Sauron. It is a testament to the instinctive genius of the writer that this minor episode would prove to become so multi-layered in the context of the entire history of Middle-earth and the War of the Ring. It raised the question of how much we, as readers, illustrators, or film-makers could ignore all those further ramifications when returning to the world of *The Hobbit*.

Gollum's character, even in his first appearance, is appealingly ambiguous. He is malevolent, self-serving and murderous, but also possessed of some vestigial sense of honour and willingness to abide by the rules of fair play. He is a strikingly original creation, though with some similarities to characters from European folklore.

One of the pleasures for me in working on the 'Riddles in the Dark' scenes for the film was the design for Gollum's boat; it seemed logical that he would build it himself, as a coracle with locally sourced materials: the hides and bones of some of his goblin victims.

## Frying-Pan

Tolkien based much of his descriptions of the Misty Mountains on a walking tour of the Swiss Alps. The Aletsch Glacier provided some memorable moments of boulders, released by thawing snow, rolling across the narrow footpath he was following, and of sliding down a scree slope, which became a model for the hurried exit from the goblin caves. For the film, we created small sets of footpaths and forested slopes which were shot against green screen and later blended into the wider computer-generated environments. Both John Howe and I had stayed on after principal photography, when the need for physical sets had ceased, to work on these and other environments, and assist in the design of all those action sequences that ensured our heroes wouldn't have too many dull moments.

## Frying-Pan

Tolkien based much of his descriptions of the Misty Mountains on a walking tour of the Swiss Alps. The Aletsch Glacier provided some memorable moments of boulders, released by thawing snow, rolling across the narrow footpath he was following, and of sliding down a scree slope, which became a model for the hurried exit from the goblin caves. For the film, we created small sets of footpaths and forested slopes which were shot against green screen and later blended into the wider computer-generated environments. Both John Howe and I had stayed on after principal photography, when the need for physical sets had ceased, to work on these and other environments, and assist in the design of all those action sequences that ensured our heroes wouldn't have too many dull moments.

Everything had to be meticulously planned through the Pre-visualisation (or 'Pre-vis') department, under Christian Rivers, and care taken to ensure that all the designers, and the Stunt, Movement Design and Motion Capture teams, were working in concert. The use of 3D and a higher frame rate also imposed new disciplines and provided more work for the crews and compositors.

Helicopters were used extensively (and enjoyably) for location recces and the gathering of photographic reference for matte and texture painting for the Middle-earth landscapes we were creating. Although this world can be thought of as a fantasy, we wanted it to look as real as possible and for the backgrounds to even fully digital shots to look as if they were of the same raw material as scenes shot on location.

# WILDERLAND

The eagles leave the travellers on the Carrock, a towering island of rock in the Anduin river, and on the border of Beorn's territory – most likely out of respect for a being as ancient and mysterious as themselves. This domain comprises the rich farmland he cares for and the wider tracts of land he guards in his bear-shape.

John and I provided many drawings of potential homes for this enigmatic being and his animal companions, ranging from one which was half-house and half-cave, to various types of timbered hall, stone farmhouse and outbuildings.

One version, designed to fit in with a potential location on a high and rocky fell, resembled a medieval hall house, similar to some of the thatched cottages I know on Dartmoor, in which the animal and human quarters are on either side of a central hall.

I think of Beorn as an ageless character, with a deep understanding of the natural world, and thought one way of expressing this would be in the form of carvings throughout his dwelling showing the evolution and variety of animal life.

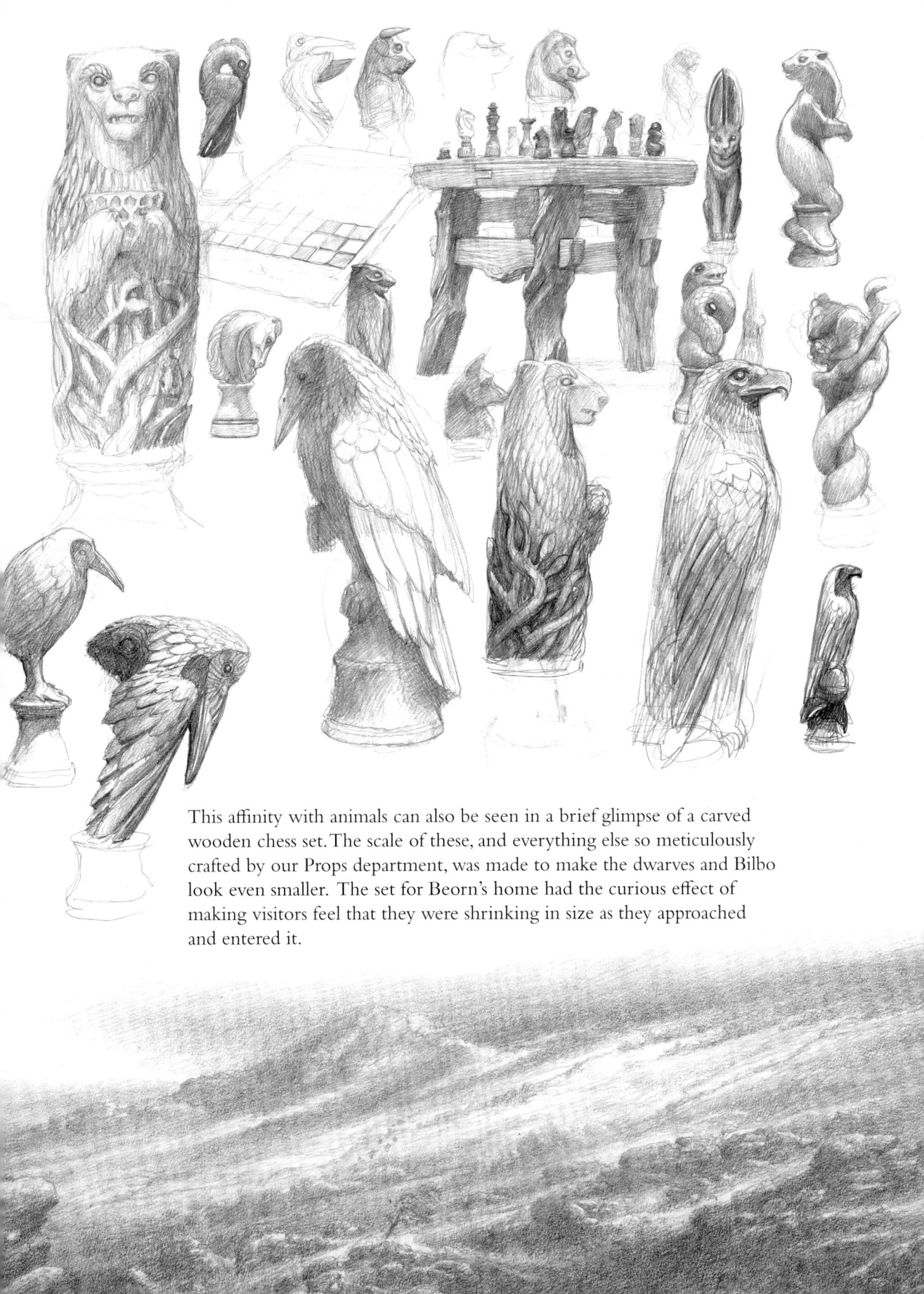

This affinity with animals can also be seen in a brief glimpse of a carved wooden chess set. The scale of these, and everything else so meticulously crafted by our Props department, was made to make the dwarves and Bilbo look even smaller. The set for Beorn's home had the curious effect of making visitors feel that they were shrinking in size as they approached and entered it.

The Forest of Mirkwood, once Greenwood the Great – full of life and dappled sunlight, but now dark and blighted – is Tolkien's version of the mysterious forests of European romance and fairy-tale, a labyrinth of unknown perils, temptations and adventures. It is inevitable that those who enter will, at some point, no matter how clear the instructions to stay on the path, become lost and entrapped.

I love walking in woodland, and painting and drawing trees more than anything else; the process of being lost in a maze of my own making for a few days is very beguiling. I draw from nature as much as possible, returning to my studio with sketches and mind full of textures and forms of roots and branches, and then – beginning with a few randomly placed lines – start to invent an imaginary forest. Even a small study of a piece of ivy-bound wood – my garden and studio being full of such things – if carefully observed, will lend some veracity to the larger trees and woodland I'm drawing.

The idea that the health of the forest had suffered under the malign influence of the Necromancer, the trees choked and dying under infestations of parasites, thorns and fungi, guided the construction and dressing of the sets made for the film. In watercolour, I use salt sprinkled into the wash and a fine brush to get the effect of lichen and other growths; on the set we were throwing handfuls of a mix of sawdust, paint and shellac at the trees and rocks to get a similar effect on a larger scale. By intensifying the colour of fungi and other growths and rotted wood we tried to add a hallucinogenic quality to the Company's journey.

We designed spores that would drift through the airless gloom, and also explored the idea that the deer may be seen almost as apparitions, with a faerie quality that would only be revealed as they turned: seen as living creatures from one angle, but composed of twigs and leaf litter when viewed from another.

# Radagast

Radagast the Brown, though one of Mirkwood's more benign inhabitants, is one of the Maiar, who along with Gandalf, Saruman and two Blue Wizards has come to Middle-earth in human form to counter the influence of Sauron. Although only mentioned briefly in *The Hobbit* book, the opportunity to represent Gandalf's cousin – as he refers to his fellow wizard – was eagerly taken up by the film's designers.

The little that is known about him – that he has a special connection with birds and beasts, and only reluctantly ventures far from his beloved forest to involve himself in the lives of humans and elves – suggests a hermit-like existence. The improvised and home-made clothing and a relaxed attitude to personal hygiene, with infestations of mice in his robes and bird's nests in his hair, were artistic licence.

# Rhosgobel

The need for an equally individual home for Radagast was also met with a variety of designs by myself and John. We agreed that it should be built in or around a tree, and loved Peter's idea that a sapling in the wall when it was first built had by now become a fully grown and ancient oak, pushing the bisected house out of shape.

All the furniture would have been made by Radagast from fallen wood and other found material. No living trees would have been cut down to provide timber, and his scientific instruments would be similarly improvised.

In drawing these buildings I'm only partially thinking about the story and the requirements of the script and the set building. I must admit that a large part of the process is in placing myself in those circumstances, and in the kind of surroundings that give me most pleasure and a sense of peace, or creative quiet. The natural and built environments should reflect the personality of their inhabitants and give clues to his or her history, but they are also the result of a fascination and an imaginative exploration, and if it is of a place you would like to live in – at least for a while – then the pleasure is multiplied.

## Dol Guldur

The other side of that creative coin is in imagining the most disturbing and hazardous places, such as Dol Guldur. This is an equally fascinating process and draws on different aspects of one's own personality, fears and repulsions. A visual language is developed, mainly of sharp, angular and gestural lines, of pitted stone and rusted metal, thorny snake-like vines and bone-filled cages.

Finding visual motifs that can be repeated in various forms adds a unity to the whole thing, making it instantly recognizable. The central courtyard is where much of the action takes place and was where we started the design work. I based the design on a triangle, with the three sides giving access via chevron-shaped steps to where the nine Ringwraiths would appear. This arrangement, applied to flagstones, facades, plinths and arches, meant that every view would have an unsettling, angular quality.

Repeating patterns allowed us to build the extensive computer-generated (or 'CG') model using a modular system, with less time needing to be spent on the components. One complete tower was built for the interior of the fortress and variations created by ruining it to different degrees, some reducing it to a stump and some hollowing out whole sides of the building. Varying the heights and swapping or rotating the towers

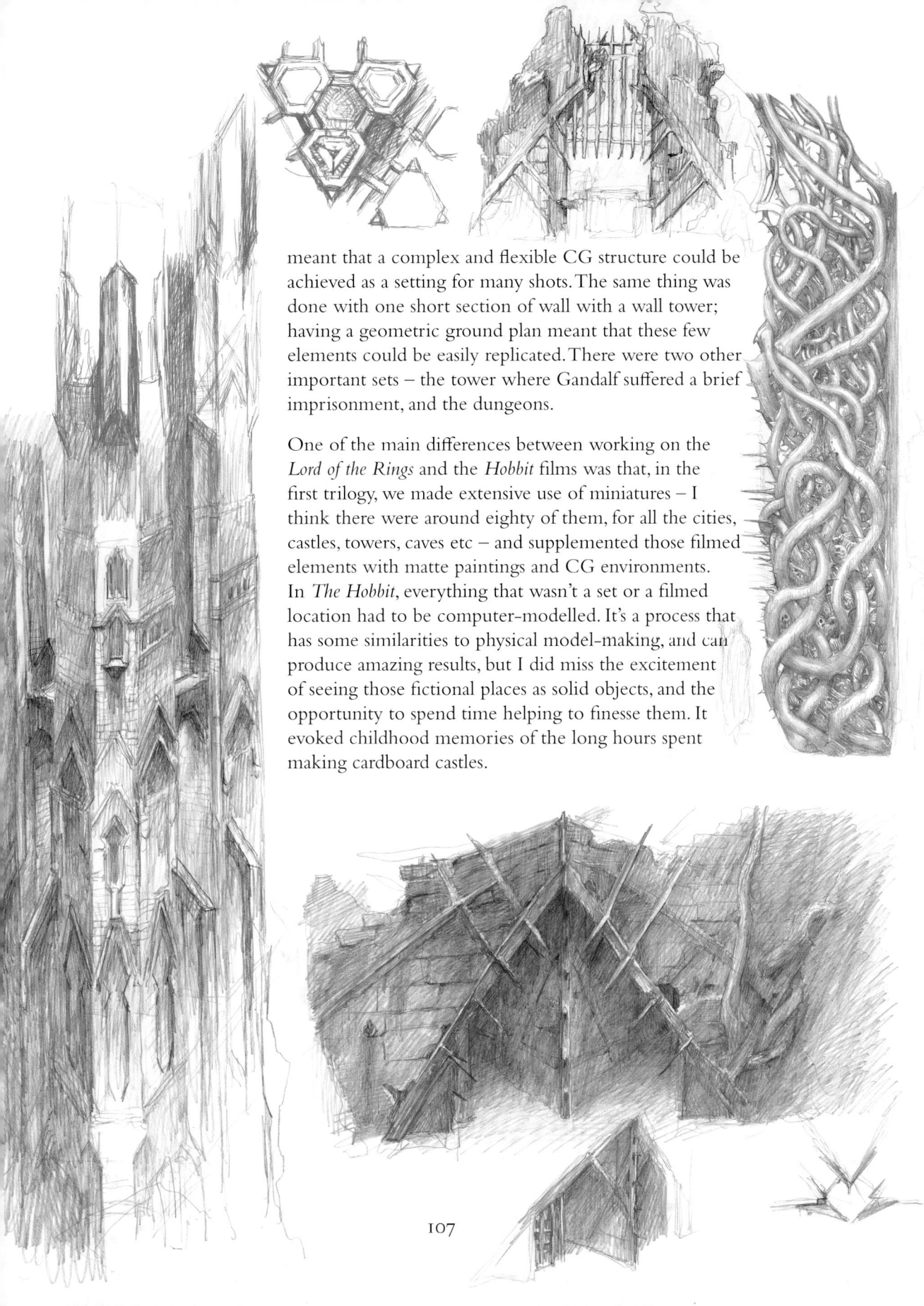

meant that a complex and flexible CG structure could be achieved as a setting for many shots. The same thing was done with one short section of wall with a wall tower; having a geometric ground plan meant that these few elements could be easily replicated. There were two other important sets – the tower where Gandalf suffered a brief imprisonment, and the dungeons.

One of the main differences between working on the *Lord of the Rings* and the *Hobbit* films was that, in the first trilogy, we made extensive use of miniatures – I think there were around eighty of them, for all the cities, castles, towers, caves etc – and supplemented those filmed elements with matte paintings and CG environments. In *The Hobbit*, everything that wasn't a set or a filmed location had to be computer-modelled. It's a process that has some similarities to physical model-making, and can produce amazing results, but I did miss the excitement of seeing those fictional places as solid objects, and the opportunity to spend time helping to finesse them. It evoked childhood memories of the long hours spent making cardboard castles.

Models were still being made in the *Hobbit* Art Department, which is where John and I were based during filming before we moved to Weta Digital for post-production. The design team, under production designer Dan Hennah, made scale versions of all the sets in order to judge how they would work in the studio and, most importantly, to get a sign-off or feedback from Peter.

We had to be aware of how he was thinking about the scenes at any moment; how the convolutions of the story might be morphing. It was a very dynamic and flexible process and we needed to be continually ready with our pencils to respond to new and exciting challenges.

## Enchanted Stream

While Gandalf and the White Council are in southern Mirkwood dealing with the Necromancer, the dwarves and Bilbo are in the dark depths of the northern forest struggling to stay on the Elf–path, and facing other dangers. Crossing the stream without coming into contact with the water proved too difficult for Bombur, who falls into a deep sleep and has to be carried for several days.

We built two sets for Mirkwood as seen at ground level, flooding part of the larger of these to create the Enchanted Stream, and making as many routes through and around it as possible, to create new settings for all the travelling shots and other scenes.

Our previous experience of creating believable Middle-earth forests in sheds in Wellington seemed fairly straightforward in comparison to filling the largest soundstage with these huge, rotting trees, festooned with garishly coloured fungi and ropes of ivy. We had a small separate set for Bilbo emerging through the canopy, to see how much further they have to go, and another for the spider's nest where the dwarves are bound up and hanging in cocoons of spider thread.

The capture of Bilbo's companions by huge spiders in the depths of Mirkwood, and his successful rescue attempt is, for me, one of the most enjoyable passages in the book – and a pleasure to draw. The image of a dozen semi-conscious figures wrapped in cocoons of spider silk, and suspended in the trees, recognizable only by the occasional protruding nose or foot, is delightfully surreal and memorable.

Spiders seem to be a source of fascination for the author, and these ones must be descendants of Ungoliant, the gigantic creature who destroyed the trees of the Valar and tried to ensnare the Sun, along with another favourite of mine – Shelob.

With courage, cunning and the aid of his magic ring, Bilbo frees the dwarves and leads the spiders away, only to see them captured again by the Wood-elves, who had beguiled them away from the footpath with the prospect of food – the dwarves having long since exhausted their supplies. Bilbo follows the captives into the underground realm of the Elvenking.

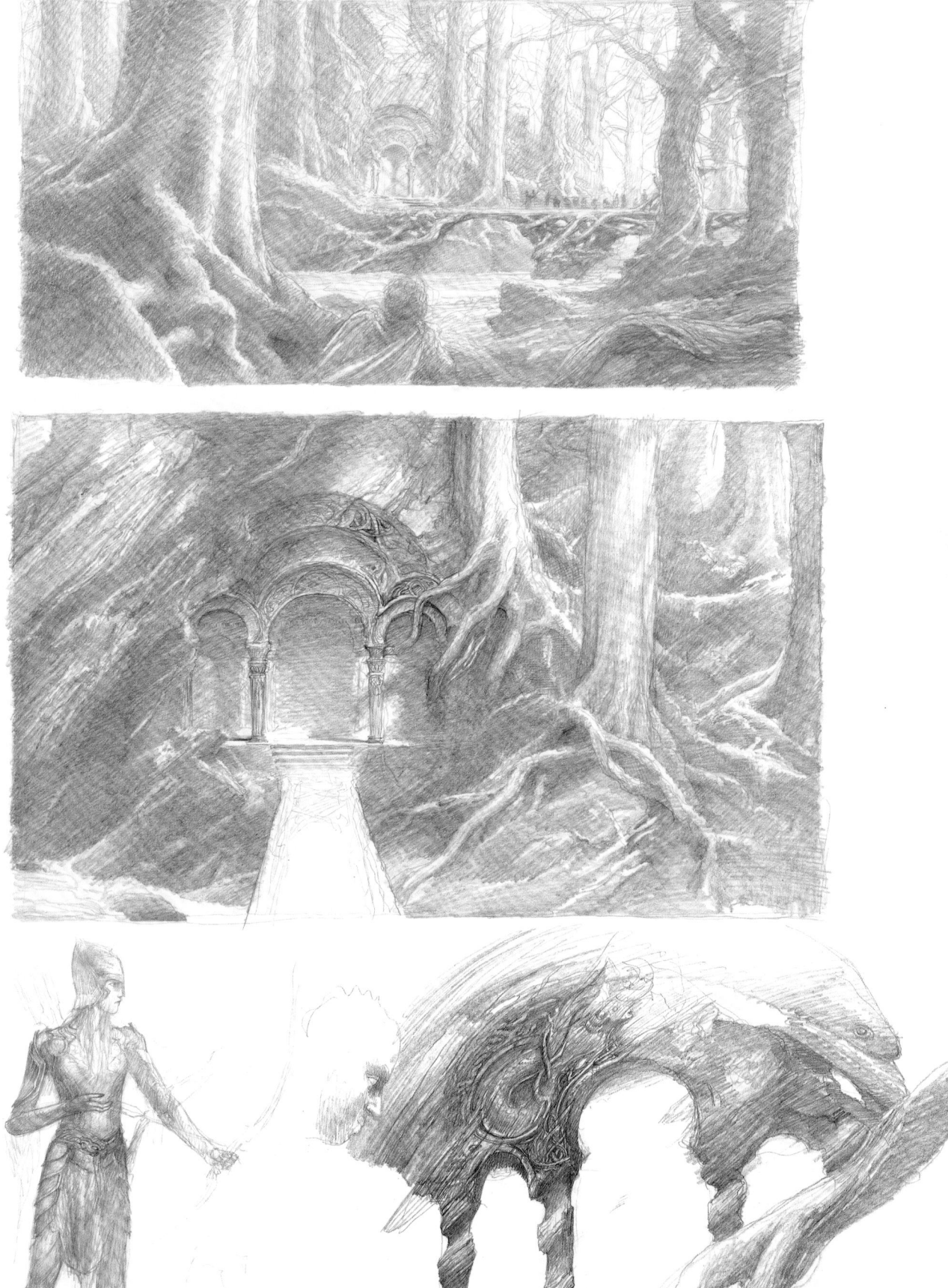

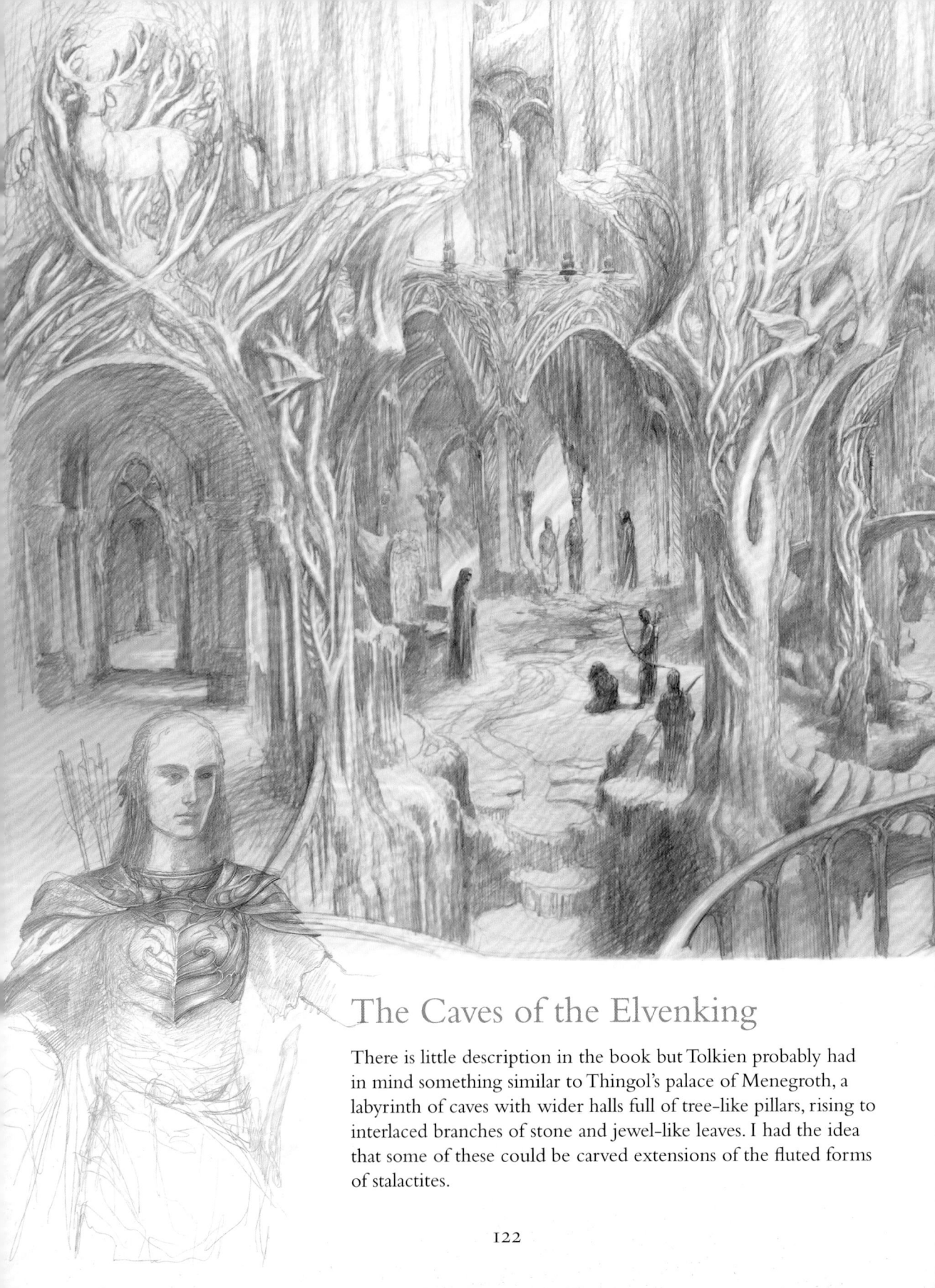

## The Caves of the Elvenking

There is little description in the book but Tolkien probably had in mind something similar to Thingol's palace of Menegroth, a labyrinth of caves with wider halls full of tree-like pillars, rising to interlaced branches of stone and jewel-like leaves. I had the idea that some of these could be carved extensions of the fluted forms of stalactites.

The Wood-elves are undoubtedly less hospitable than their counterparts in Rivendell and Lothlórien, and have long memories and a list of grievances against the dwarves, including for the sacking of Menegroth thousands of years previously.

We wanted this hostile edge to be reflected in their décor and costumes, adding sharp thorn- or antler-like shapes to the distinctive flowing lines that are typical of elven style. This would be especially apparent in designs for their weapons and armour.

Thranduil's throne, as we see it on film, is set in the centre of the largest cavern, at the highest point, so that he has a commanding view of the whole environment – a highly decorated forest of stone. As an additional touch, the roots of some of the larger trees on the hill above extend as serpentine forms into the cave, and one forms the base of the throne.

Feasting seems to be an important part of elven life and there was a point in the film's development where we had planned to see more of the celebratory side of their nature. We commissioned an excellent ceramicist, glass-blowers and silversmiths to make tableware, and even devised entertainment in the form of a series of tableaux to mock Thorin and his imprisoned companions.

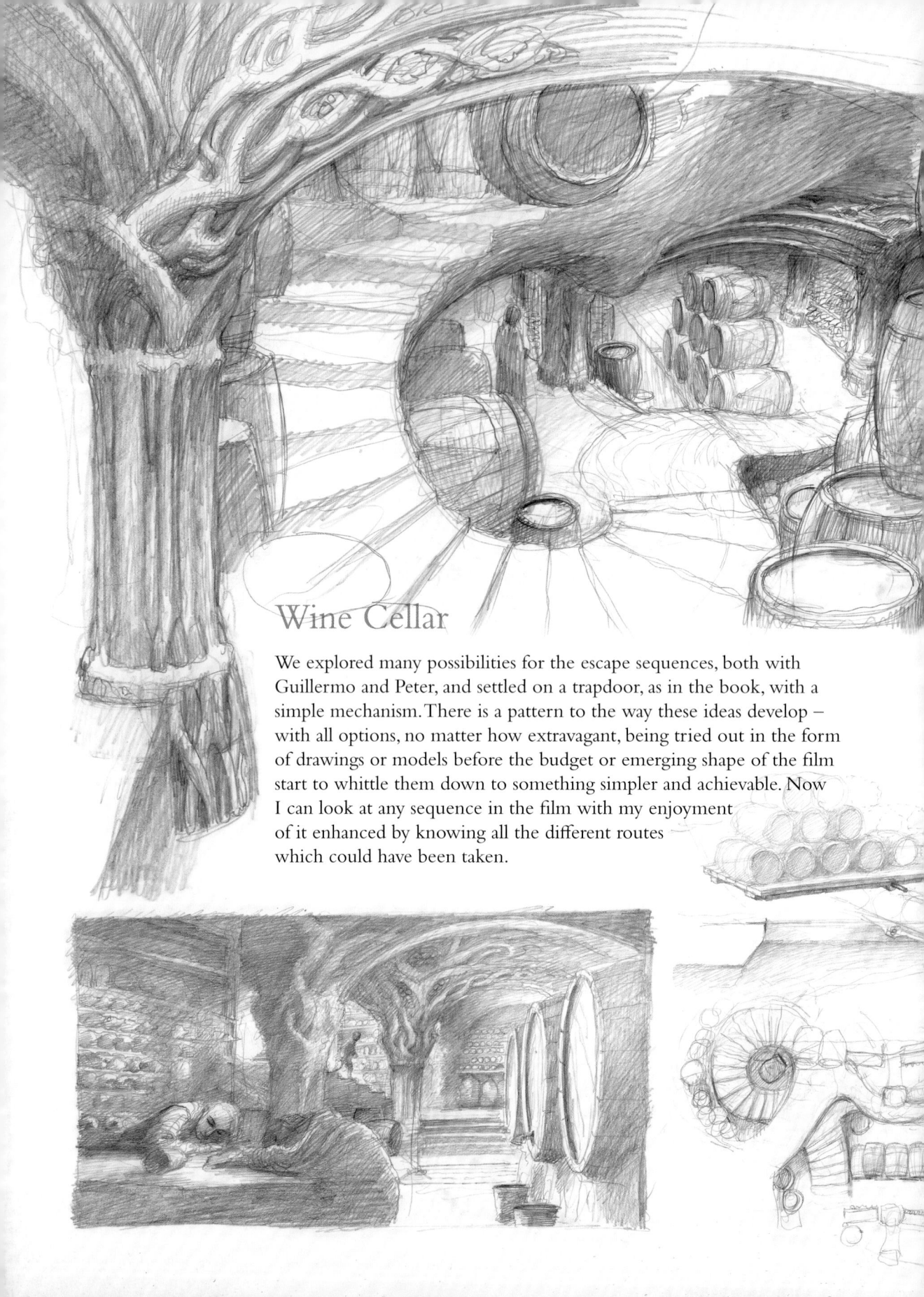

# Wine Cellar

We explored many possibilities for the escape sequences, both with Guillermo and Peter, and settled on a trapdoor, as in the book, with a simple mechanism. There is a pattern to the way these ideas develop – with all options, no matter how extravagant, being tried out in the form of drawings or models before the budget or emerging shape of the film start to whittle them down to something simpler and achievable. Now I can look at any sequence in the film with my enjoyment of it enhanced by knowing all the different routes which could have been taken.

Bilbo persuades the freed dwarves to hide in the barrels which are to be returned to Lake-town. These are then cast into the stream that flows beneath the Elvenking's palace, and through a water-gate into the Forest River. Bilbo has a first sighting of the Lonely Mountain when the river, emerging from the forested hills, spreads and slows through an area of marshland.

Knowing that Lake-town is built around the ruins of an earlier and grander city, that it is blighted and run-down, and ruled by a corrupt and selfish Master, gave us the cues we needed for this series of sets. Ideas about architectural style evolved but we eventually settled on a look that hints at eastern Europe, with shingle-roofed wooden buildings and decorative facades and gables. The overall impression is of a city slowly subsiding into the water, its timber and piles warped and rotting. The sets were a delight to explore, with houses, market places, chandlers and many types of fishing boat. Dan Hennah had been a trawler captain before taking up art direction, so he took a particular interest in making all the vessels workable. Set dressers, crew and actors had to take care when moving about as the three large sets were all sitting in a couple of feet of water.

The most important building serves as town hall, treasury and the dwelling of the Master of Lake-town, wonderfully played by Stephen Fry. It was also one of my favourite sets – small, complete and beautifully dressed, it was a credit to all the construction crew, carpenters, sculptors, painters and set dressers who worked so hard and to such good effect.

Peter likes to give as many of the backroom crew as possible a chance to step briefly into the limelight and have a cameo in the films. I had done so twice in the *Lord of the Rings* films, and John and I were invited to dress in heraldic outfits and become members of the band that played an off-key fanfare as the Company departs Lake-town. We had both designed instruments, with little regard for how easy they would be to handle – and mine weighed about three times as much as I had expected – so there was poetic, if not musical, justice done that day.

# Dale & Erebor

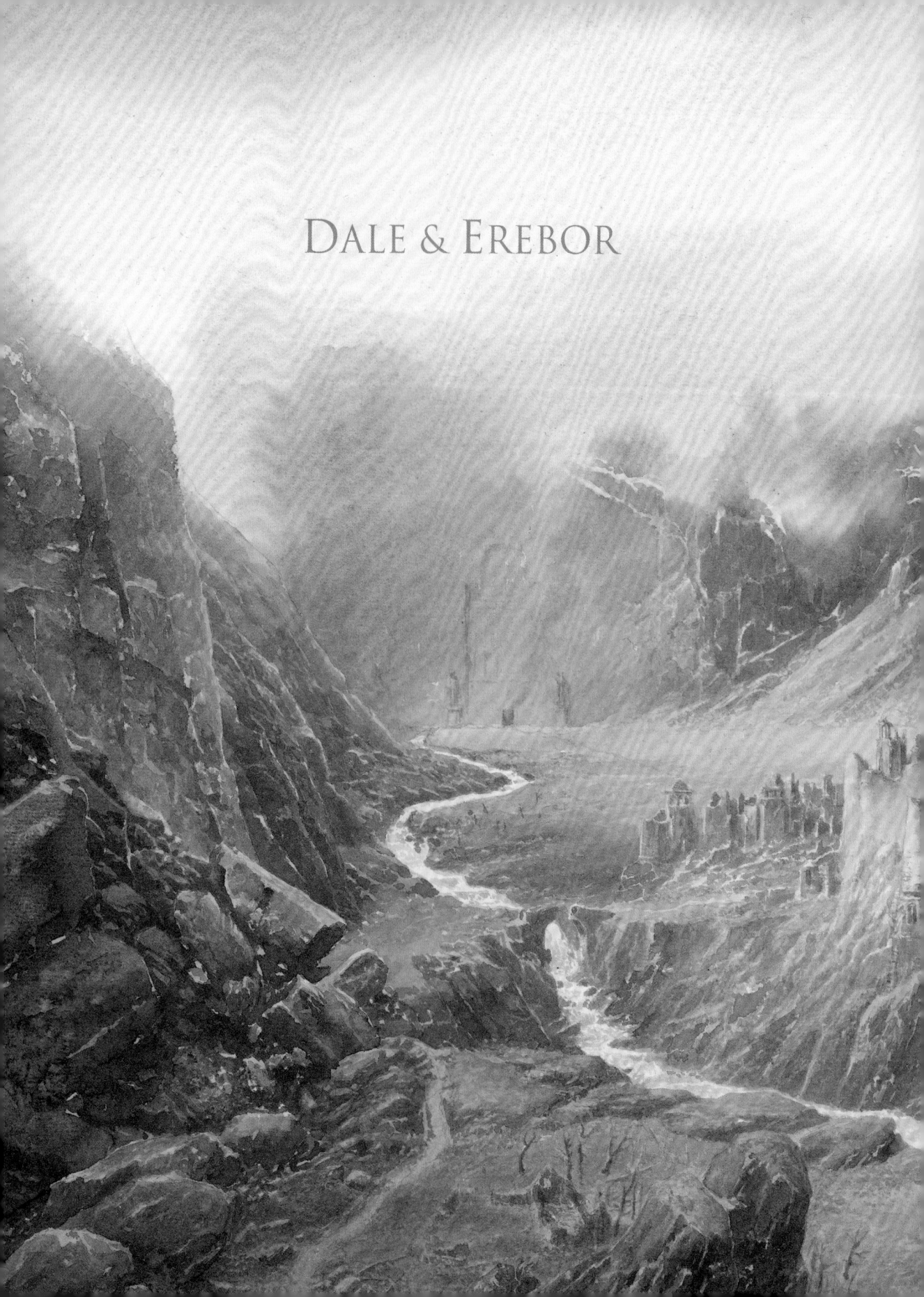

One of the first things we do when starting work on a new environment is to make a map or a bird's eye view, showing the topography and rough placement of landscape features and buildings. At this stage, it's just for discussion, when all the possibilities for future action are being considered. I placed a small lake in the valley between Dale and Erebor, thinking that if it were to freeze over, there might be potential for some of the battle taking place on ice (having been impressed by the ice battle in Eisenstein's *Alexander Nevsky*).

Dale had to be conceived both as a ruin, as part of the desolation of Smaug, and as a city in its prime – full of life and colour, with markets and gardens, as we see it prior to the dragon's attack. We built the set on a nearby hillside overlooking Wellington's harbour, first as a beautiful city; then, after two days of shooting, the construction crew returned to trash all their fine work, filling the streets with rubble and reducing the upper stories of the buildings to scorched and broken timbers.

The set wasn't vast – a couple of gateways, a section of rampart, a courtyard with the frontage of the great hall and a little warren of streets and alleyways, and an elevated walkway – but there was enough variety of views that it was able to be used for a large number of shots, giving the impression of a much larger city.

After getting a rough overview, based on the author's descriptions and anything the director may have said, I will start with a sketch, perhaps of a gateway, and then imagine myself under that archway looking up the street. Having drawn that, I find a spot within that drawing from which to imagine further views, each successive drawing bringing me closer to having an imaginary city in my head, and in my sketchbooks.

These may need to be changed as the whole thing crystallizes, and as ideas are shared and provoke feedback. Then models are made from individual building designs and the final shape is pinned down by the director as he plans shots and action sequences. This is followed by numerous drawings of details of windows, door handles, sculptures, murals – everything that will be needed to make the set complete and convincing.

Tolkien's own drawings and maps, and his descriptions, are studied carefully and will always be a first point of reference even if the detail of the drama is following a different course. One way in which the films may vary from the book is that there is a natural tendency to compress distances and journey times in order to keep the action flowing and, sometimes, to be able to see where we are going. It's also good to avoid having too many shots of characters trudging through landscapes.

The need for an overview or a plan applied to our underground kingdoms too, even though we could never see the whole thing in one shot. It is useful to know how the various tunnels, shafts, vast halls, treasure chambers and mine workings relate to one another.

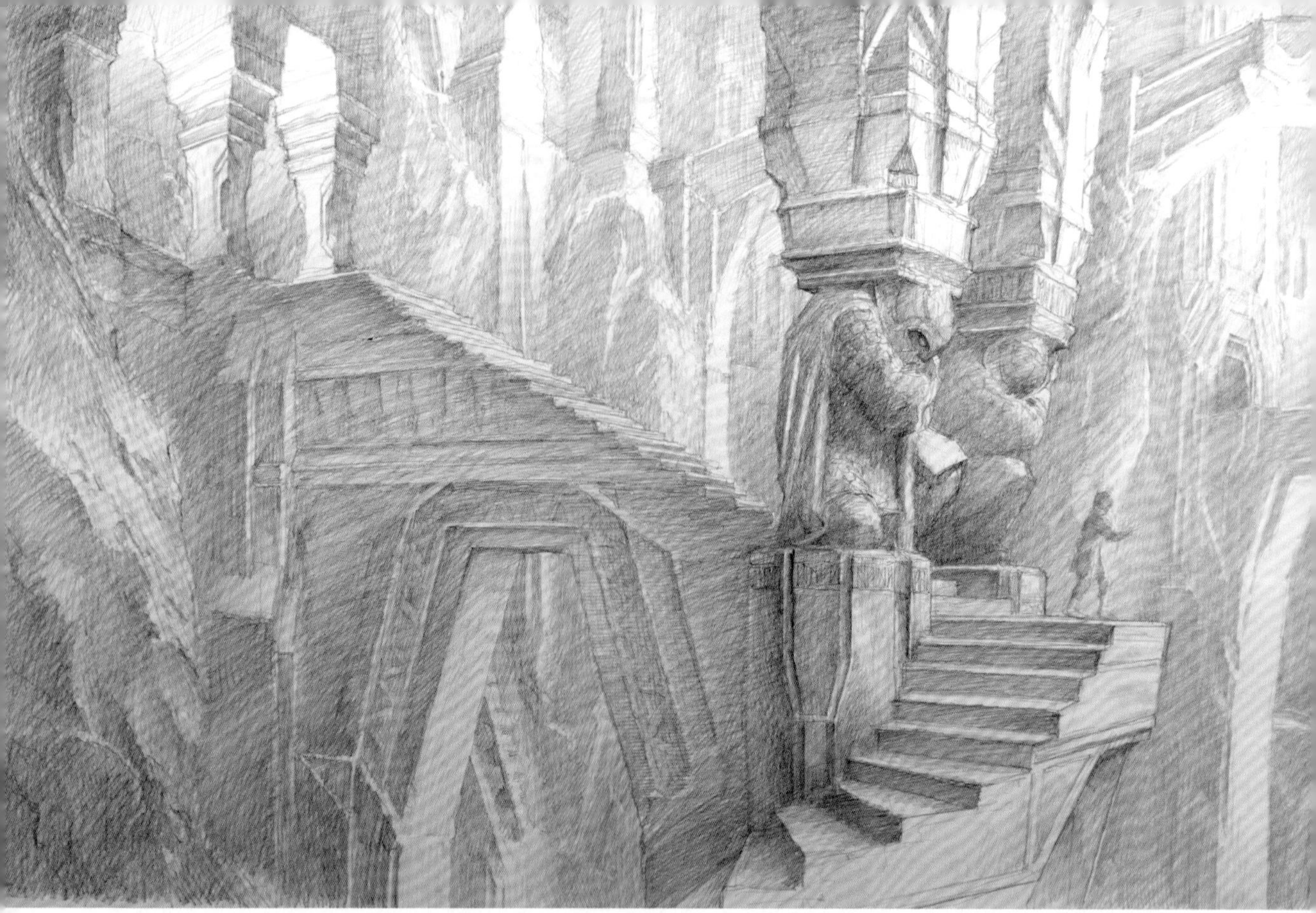

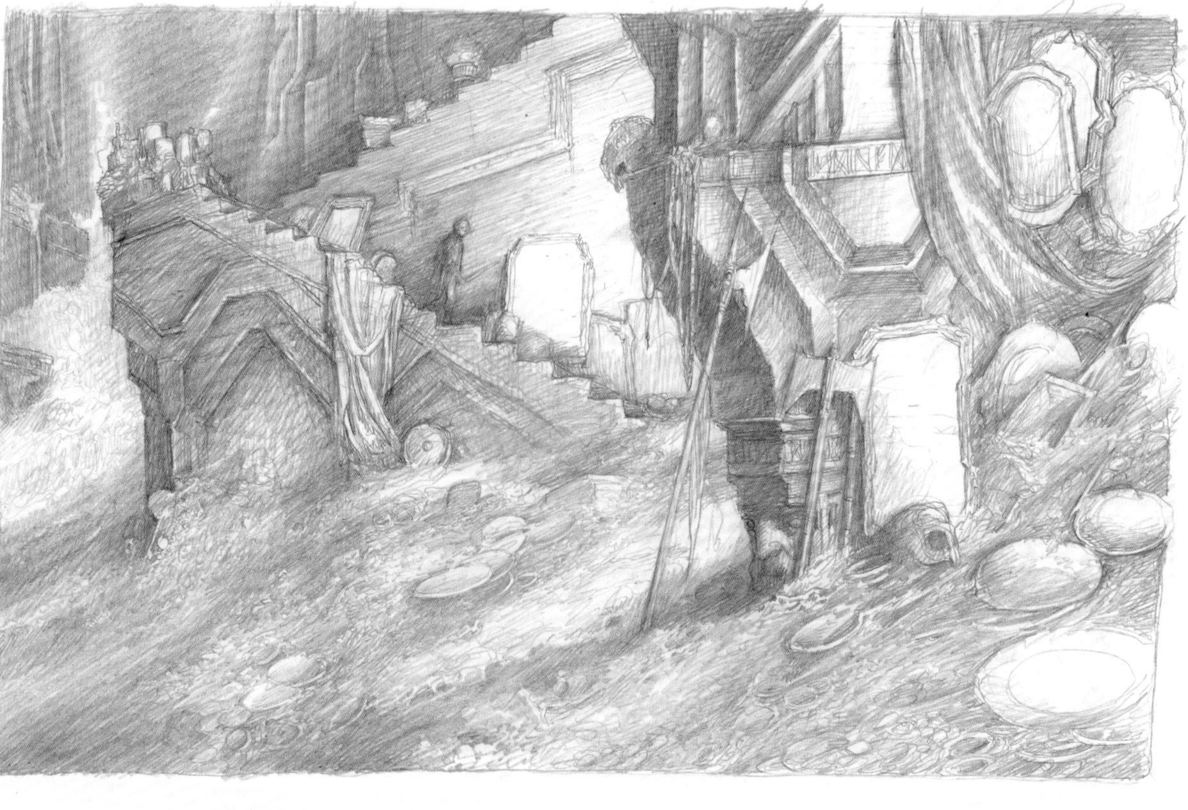

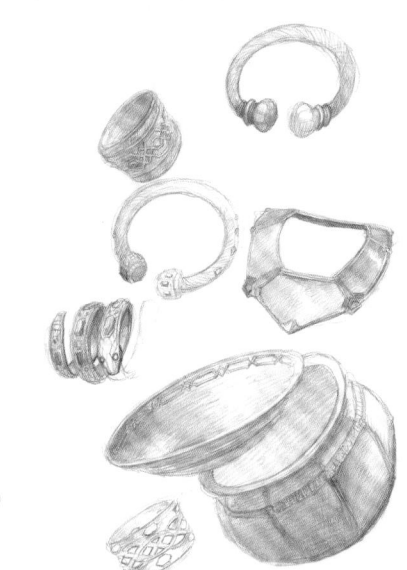

Stories of treasure-guarding dragons are ancient and widespread. Perhaps the best models for Smaug are Fáfnir, a man transformed by his own greed and crimes into a great, malignant worm, until slain by Sigurd the Völsung; and the dragon that kills Beowulf on his final quest. Bilbo can't match these great heroes in strength, but saves himself with the aid of the magic ring and his quick wits.

I have drawn quite a number of dragons over the years. My especial love of Greek, Norse and Welsh legends has brought me into regular contact with them, and the corners of my sketchbooks are alive with their serpentine forms. The combination of intelligence and malice is endlessly fascinating. Tolkien has created some of the most memorable in all literature, and of these Smaug is perhaps his most awe-inspiring addition to the canon.

# Bard & Smaug

The other heroic figure in this part of the story is Bard the Bowman. As a descendant of Girion of Dale, he is able to understand the language of birds and receives information from Bilbo's helpful thrush about the gap in the dragon's jewelled armour. His last shot, with the Black Arrow, ends Smaug's reign of terror.

I felt there was a change of tone from this point in the story. The dangers faced on the journey, though terrifying at times, were leavened with a comic element. We are still in the same extraordinary fairy-tale world, with elves, wizards, dwarves and talking animals, but with the destruction of Lake-town and the plight of its inhabitants, the increasing possessiveness and anger of Thorin, and the moral choices of Bilbo, there is now an extra dimension and gravity to the story.

The monster is dead, but the curse of the golden hoard lingers, as it does in the great ring myths of Scandinavia and Germany. It is inevitable that the ownership of that mound of treasure should be disputed and old grievances aired, as armies of men from Lake-town, elves from Mirkwood, dwarves from the Iron Hills and the massed ranks of goblins and Wargs converge on the Lonely Mountain.

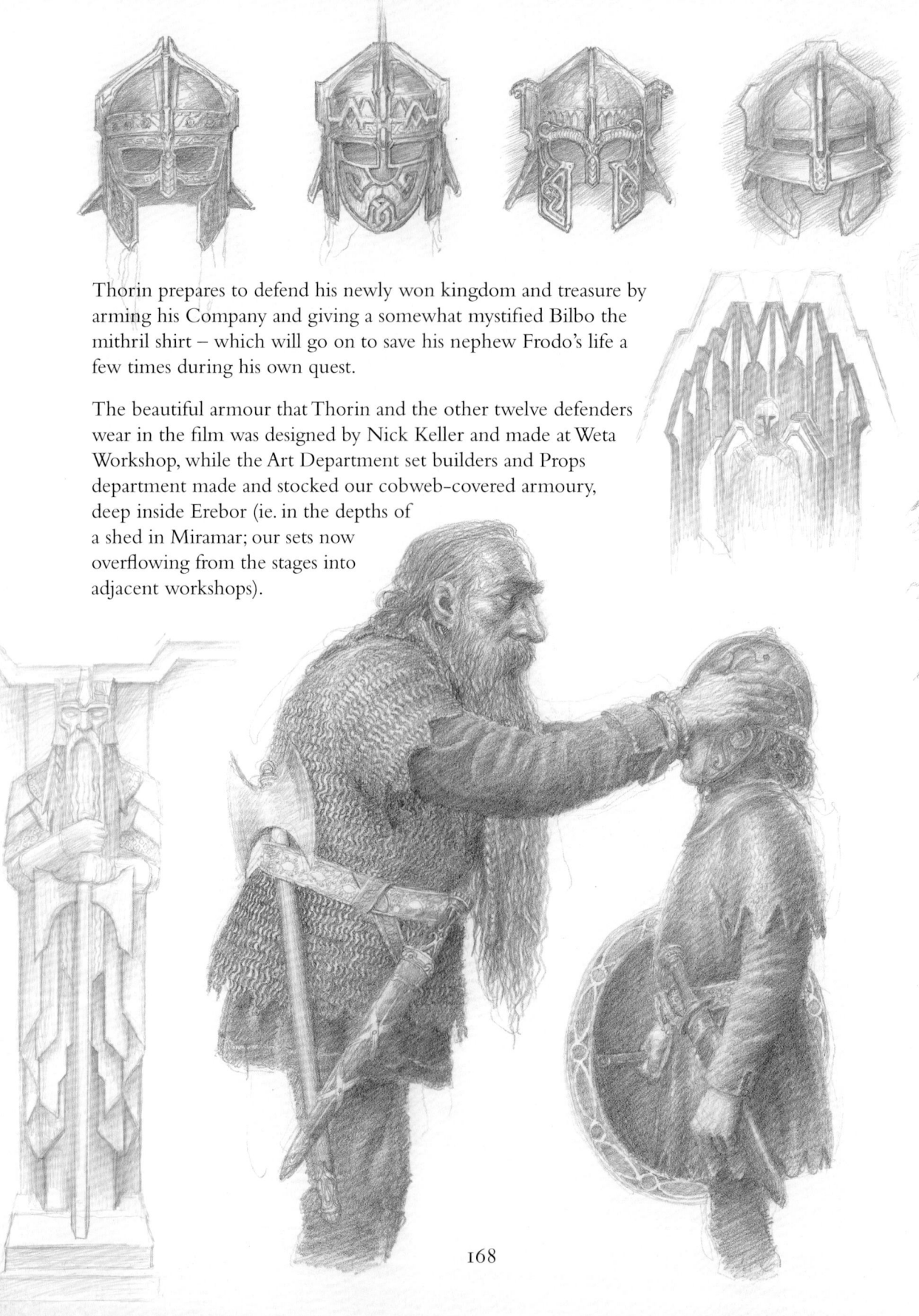

Thorin prepares to defend his newly won kingdom and treasure by arming his Company and giving a somewhat mystified Bilbo the mithril shirt – which will go on to save his nephew Frodo's life a few times during his own quest.

The beautiful armour that Thorin and the other twelve defenders wear in the film was designed by Nick Keller and made at Weta Workshop, while the Art Department set builders and Props department made and stocked our cobweb-covered armoury, deep inside Erebor (ie. in the depths of a shed in Miramar; our sets now overflowing from the stages into adjacent workshops).

Most of what we see of Erebor's interior in the films are CG extensions to small foreground sets. We had built some pillar bases, archways and sections of wall, all painted to look like green marble, which we could configure into endless variations for our action. Peter was keen to see plunging depths into forges and mines, and many levels of halls and living accommodation.

We needed to become even more flexible while in post-production on *The Desolation of Smaug*, as Peter had found a new way of shooting the angles he wanted in virtual reality. He would be moving around the motion capture stage with a camera, and in the interior of Erebor at the same time.

The largest set we built for Erebor was for the entrance hall, with the Front Gate, the bridge and flooded moat and the bottom of the improvised wall. The top of the rampart, from which Thorin defies Bard, Thranduil and their besieging troops, was a smaller separate set. Like many of the sets, the entrance hall was made in both pre- and post-Smaug states.

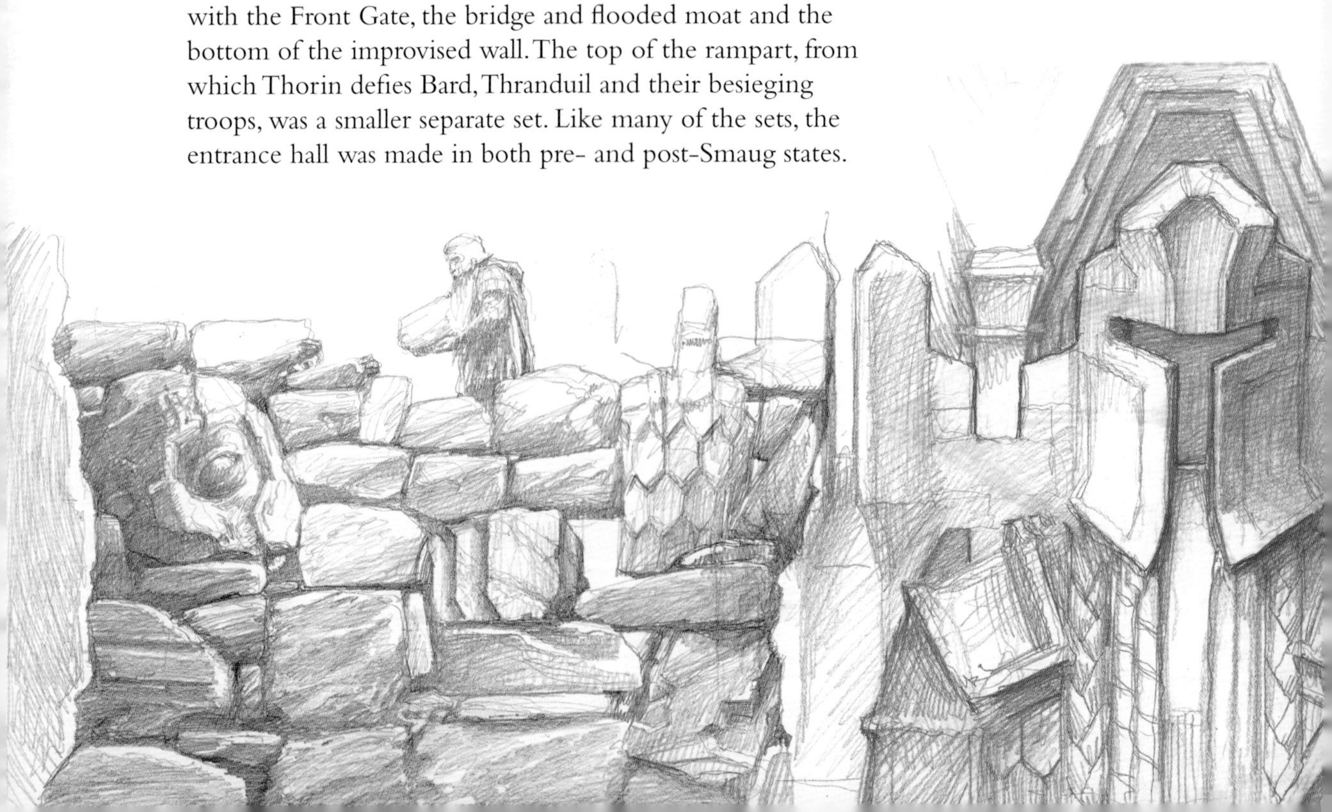

Most of what we see of Erebor's interior in the films are CG extensions to small foreground sets. We had built some pillar bases, archways and sections of wall, all painted to look like green marble, which we could configure into endless variations for our action. Peter was keen to see plunging depths into forges and mines, and many levels of halls and living accommodation.

We needed to become even more flexible while in post-production on *The Desolation of Smaug*, as Peter had found a new way of shooting the angles he wanted in virtual reality. He would be moving around the motion capture stage with a camera, and in the interior of Erebor at the same time.

The largest set we built for Erebor was for the entrance hall, with the Front Gate, the bridge and flooded moat and the bottom of the improvised wall. The top of the rampart, from which Thorin defies Bard, Thranduil and their besieging troops, was a smaller separate set. Like many of the sets, the entrance hall was made in both pre- and post-Smaug states.

A typical workday while filming *The Hobbit* would involve drawing whatever was due to be built or made in the coming weeks, and frequently switching between several different environments, props or cultural artefacts. The sketches were not what we would think of as highly finished. They would be taken to the point that they communicate what is needed to take the design process to the next stage, and then followed up with more detailed drawings or alternative views as they were required. A good part of the day would be spent working in Photoshop. Shots that have been edited into the film have their green-screen backgrounds replaced with painting, landscape reference photos or whatever is needed to show what the final shot should look like. There would be frequent discussions at Weta Workshop and with the matte painters and layout artists and modellers at Weta Digital.

During the early days of production there would be a daily meeting with Peter, or Guillermo before him, but Peter's time was more limited while shooting, and we would go onto set with a pile of drawings and a model or two, waiting for a short break in the shooting during which Dan, John and myself would crowd into the director's tent and quickly show him what we'd been doing and get his stamp of approval, or enough feedback to keep us going for a few more days.

## The Battle of Five Armies

There would also be some thinktank meetings at which people from Weta, Pre-vis, the stunt and movement choreographers and ourselves would brainstorm ideas for some of the more complex sequences. There were a lot of these around the subjects of Ravenhill, the activities within Erebor and the battle outside the Front Gate, when Dain and his Iron Hills army arrives and battle begins.

With such a large number of protagonists and creatures, varieties of orcs, ogres and trolls, bats and eagles, it would be easy to get lost in a massive and highly surreal melee and for the viewer to get confused. However, if the environment and characters have been well enough established, with the viewer knowing where they are and who is who at any given moment, this can be avoided. One way of ensuring that the viewer can follow what is going on is to keep the armies in more or less orderly ranks. We spent some time coming up with tactics and ideas for the dwarves' shield wall, and a signalling system to enable the orc commander to control his forces.

Thorin and Company finally burst out of Erebor in a 'V' formation, a spearhead to drive into the massed orcs. When I positioned the broken head of a giant statue in front of Erebor I thought it might feature in some stunt action, but I was pleased with the sense of pathos that it conveyed as it lay overlooking the battlefield.

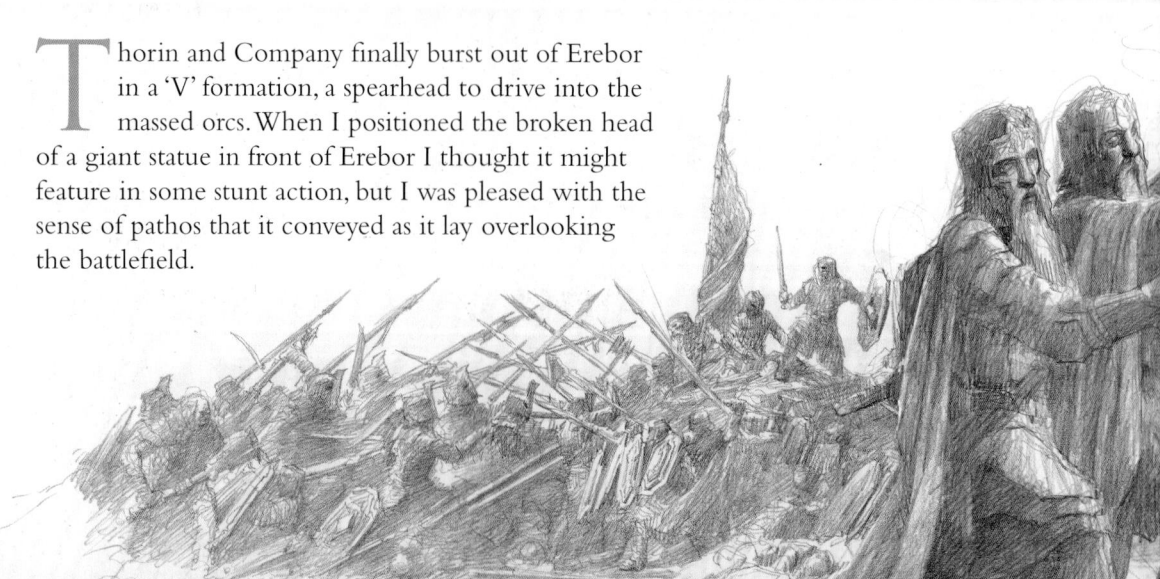

The mortal wounding of Thorin at the moment of victory, as the eagles and Beorn arrive and change the course of the battle, and the final reconciliation between him and Bilbo in the battle's aftermath, are an emotional climax to the story – made all the more powerful by the many differences between these two extraordinary personalities.

As an illustrator, whether on paper or in scenography, I realize the limits of my ability to move people compared to the more direct magic that happens when a brilliant actor holds the attention of an audience. With a few words and the subtlest of gestures he or she can transport us anywhere and to any state of mind. It is something that I have had the privilege to witness many times in working on these films, and for which I will always be grateful.

We can create the most beautifully finished, grand and atmospheric settings for these moments, and visual artists can utilize an increasingly impressive array of techniques and skills to do so, but it is when the writing and acting is at its best that all that elaborate superstructure finds a firm foundation and the magic works. All our efforts really are just shadows cast by the hands of the master storyteller.

# Going Home

In 2015, after nearly seven years of work on the *Hobbit* films – to add to the six years spent earlier on the *Lord of the Rings* trilogy – I returned to my Dartmoor home.

I had loved working on these films, and all the brilliant and beautiful souls I worked with, but I was happy to be moving back into my own home, and into the landscapes I most loved – along with the wider landscapes and ancient cities of Europe – and into the world of books again.

Fortunately, I don't have the equivalent of the Sackville-Bagginses amongst my relatives, or silver cutlery to be pilfered, so all was well when I got back home, with more stories to illustrate, and more sketchbooks to fill.

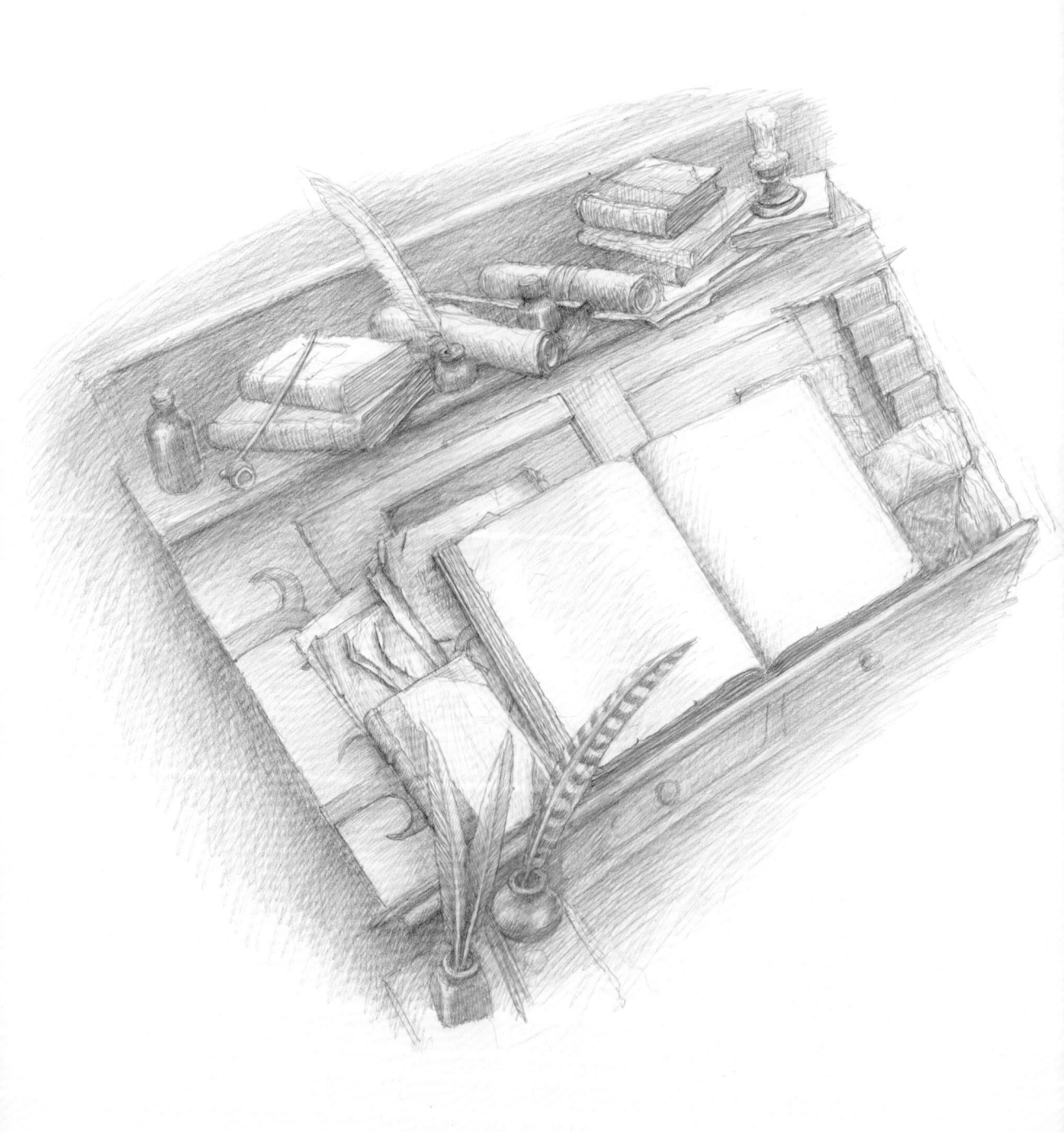

# Acknowledgements

I would like to thank Christopher and Baillie Tolkien and the Tolkien Estate for the opportunity they have given me to illustrate some of the world's finest fiction; Chris Smith and David Brawn from Harper Collins for their wisdom and support; and Marja and Virginia Lee for shouldering my responsibilities during long absences. Richard Taylor and Tania Rodger and their colleagues at Weta Workshop, Dan and Chris Hennah, Ra Vincent, Sam Genet and Kathryn Lim and everyone from the *Hobbit* Art Department, and Joe Letteri and all my friends at Weta Digital. And Guillermo del Toro, Peter Jackson and Fran Walsh, and John Howe for their kindness and inspiration.

This is a personal account of some of the processes, thoughts and adventures that *The Hobbit* has led me through as an illustrator. I haven't said too much about my responses as a reader. Every time I go back to the text my respect for the author and my enjoyment of the story is renewed, and anyone wishing for a deeper immersion in this wonderful tale would find *The History of The Hobbit*, by John D Rateliff, a truly enjoyable read.